PRETTY (IN)SIGNIFICANT

ELISABETH GARNER

Contents

Also by Elisabeth Garner   vii

Content Warning   ix

Pretty (in)Significant   xiii

Chapter 1   1

Chapter 2   5

Chapter 3   13

Chapter 4   19

Chapter 5   31

Chapter 6   39

Chapter 7   47

Chapter 8   55

Chapter 9   67

Chapter 10   75

Chapter 11   89

Chapter 12   99

Chapter 13   109

Chapter 14   123

Chapter 15   137

Chapter 16   153

Chapter 17   161

Chapter 18   177

Coming up next   193

About the Author   195

To everyone who wanted to know "the other side" of what happened at the end of Pretty Little Picture and all curious people who want to know all the behind-the-scenes info.

Matt and Chickadee - I love you two so much! Thank you for sharing me with the Agostis. They send their appreciation.
To my besties, Hype Girls Squad Discord, ARC team, and Readers - I would be lost without you, and my books would not be nearly as good... or filled with red string!

Also by Elisabeth Garner

The "Love Prevails" Series

(Contemporary Romance)

Even Angels Fall (#1)

Even Hearts Struggle (#2)

Even Hope Returns (#3)

The "Gorgeous, Armed, and Dangerous" Series

(Suspense Romance)

Not Just Another Pretty Face (#1)

Pretty Little Picture (#2)

Pretty (in) Significant (#2.5)

Pretty Much Screwed (#3)

Locked and Loaded - Fall 2023 (#4)

Loaded Question - Spring 2024 (#5)

Loaded Secrets - 2024 (#6)

Fatal Attraction - Release Date TBD (#7)

Fatal Consequences - Release Date TBD (#8)

Final Fate - Release Date TBD (#9)

Content Warning

Pretty (in)Significant is a suspense romance, and some elements have a mafia flair to them. That being said, there is adult content in this book, including but not limited to physical violence, gun violence, on-page death, offensive language, and non-fade to black romantic scenes.

For readers sensitive to these elements, please take note.

"If you wanted to kiss me, all you had to was ask."
   - Chelsea Turner, Pretty (in)Significant

Pretty (in)Significant

Chapter One

Phil

"Earth to Phil. You keep drooling like that, and we're going to have to call housekeeping to clean up the puddle."

I blinked, a little pissed at myself for being caught off guard like that and wiped my mouth with the back of my hand. When I found it dry, I flipped off Peter, who only chuckled. "Can I help you?"

"Well, I was going to relieve you, but if you want to stay longer I can walk over to where Chelsea went and ask her if she likes you like we're in middle school again. Or you can write her a note asking her out, I can deliver it, and she can circle yes or no."

"Shut up. I'm not afraid to talk to her. Hell, she had me carrying a couple of boxes for her earlier."

Peter just shook his head. "Anything I need to know before I start working and you continue to ogle her from across the room like a coward?"

It wasn't my fault she looked that good climbing up and down that stepladder. I took a deep breath. "Nothing to report."

Peter nodded and headed out to make his rounds, and Lukas

almost immediately walked into the Reading Room, where I still stood.

"Ryan needs to have a conversation with me, and one I can't have out in the open or with Quinn right there. I know you're off, but can you cover until I'm off this call?"

"Of course." I knew he wouldn't dawdle.

"Thank you." He headed out the door, the phone already to his ear.

It had been this chaotic since Lukas had called me and Peter out to Colorado. It didn't surprise me that he had us come out to help him keep "a friend of the family" safe from their crazy and toxic ex. That was literally part of what we did, especially for family. It *did* surprise me, though, that he'd only known this 'friend' for a week before making the call. It wasn't like Lukas to attach so strongly to a woman to the point of bringing in part of his security team, but once I saw him and Quinn together and got details about *why* we were here, it made sense.

I looked over, and Quinn was now in the lobby standing near Chelsea, helping her secure an evergreen swag to the front of the front desk. "Please? It would make me feel better. If something happened to you... I'd never forgive myself."

Interesting. I wonder what Quinn is all worked up about? I walked up to the duo. "Hello, ladies."

Without pause, Quinn turned to face me, and the over-whelming tension and concern in her blue eyes bored into mine. "Could you please do me a favor?"

I tipped my head to the side, more than curious about what had her all worked up in the short time Lukas had been away from her. "I'll do my best. What's up?"

"Can you or Peter please go with Chelsea this weekend when she goes to buy her Christmas tree? She keeps insisting she'll be fine, but I don't want anything happening to her."

After glancing at Chelsea, who seemed both hopeful and

mortified as she tried to look busy untangling some twinkle lights, I returned my attention to Quinn. "I'd be more than happy to."

Quinn let out a deep, relieved-sounding sigh. "Thank you."

"Of course."

She glanced at the clock behind the desk, then narrowed her eyes at me. "Wait, aren't you supposed to be off and going home right now?"

I nodded. "Yeah, but I told Lukas I'd stay so he could have his chat with Ryan." Quinn opened her mouth, but I cut her off. "I'm sure it will only be a few minutes. It's fine."

She shook her head. "That man. Oh well, I've got things to finish up. Let's parade over to my office." She gave Chelsea a quick hug. "Thank you for not fighting me too hard about this." With that, Quinn glanced up at me. "Ready?"

"After you."

I followed one step behind and to the right of Quinn to her office. When she got to the door, her hand froze on the handle. "I know it's probably not in your job description, or within your assignment, and if I have to talk to Lukas bef—"

"Quinn. Stop." When she did, I went on. "Like Lukas, you asked me. I could have said no. I didn't want to."

After a moment, a smirk appeared on her face. "You really like her, don't you?"

"I... What?" *How does she know? Am I not being as careful as I think?*

She snickered softly. "Don't worry. Your secret is safe with me. But seriously, if Lukas wants to give you shit about covering her for an afternoon, send him my way."

"I... Um... Thanks? And I will."

Quinn patted my arm. "Someone has to look out for you, too."

I had just finished eating dinner when my phone dinged. *Please don't let it be an emergency.* My eyes went wide when I saw the name. I had not been expecting to hear from her.

Lianne: < I'm flying in tomorrow morning to surprise Lukas. Can you get me from the airport without him finding out? >

Phil: < I'm not working in the morning. I can slip out and pick you up. Let me know what time to be there. >

Lianne forwarded her flight information, and the fact Ben was also joining her.

Why is she surprising her brother?

Chapter Two

Chelsea

I had just hung up the phone after taking down a reservation. Even after having a night to sleep it off, my feelings were still all over the place. I was still both irritated and elated that Quinn had asked Phil to come with me to get my Christmas tree. I knew I'd be fine on my own, but I would have been lying if the thought of finally being alone with him hadn't made me a little giddy.

Someone clearing their throat brought me back to the present, and I mentally scolded myself for letting *him* take over my thoughts again. When I glanced up, there was a woman with dark blond hair pulled back into a high ponytail. "Oh, hi. Welcome to Cardinal Hideaway. How can I help you?"

She smiled. "Hi. Would you happen to know where Lukas Agosti is right now? I know he's here working on some paintings for the owner."

I glanced up at Connor, who was sitting in the corner, and when he nodded at me, I nodded at her. "I believe he's painting in the Reading Room right now. If you just go through those double doors right there, you should see him set up in the corner nearest the fireplace with his easel."

She looked in the direction I gestured and then smiled at me again. "Thank you so much."

As she walked toward the Reading Room, I wanted to ask Connor if he knew who she was, but Quinn walked up to the desk before I could get the words out.

"Who was that?"

I shrugged. "Not sure. She asked where Lukas was, so I directed her to the Reading Room. Mr. Broody Guard over there didn't make a move to stop me from telling her, so I figured she was fine."

Quinn glanced at Connor, who was still sitting in one of the leather chairs near the fire with a book in his hands.

"She's fine."

Quinn furrowed her brow as she turned her attention toward the room in question.

Is she jealous or worried? I nearly snickered. "You're going to check out who's here to see your man, aren't you?"

"Chelsea!"

I shrugged. "What? I see that possessive, jealous look in your eyes. Didn't you recently call out Lukas for getting worked up because you were all chummy with his guys?"

"I don't need you and your impeccable logic right now." She let out a deep sigh as she headed toward the Reading Room. As Quinn approached the door, I faintly heard a quiet, "Can't a girl surprise her favorite guy?"

Uh oh. That is not going to go over well. My eyebrows shot up, and I looked at Connor. "Care to fill me in on who was asking about Lukas?"

"His sister."

"What?" Once again, before I could get an answer, I saw a tall man approaching the doors. *Damn. The one time I'm upset to see a guest.* I gave him my best smile as he walked in. "Welcome to Cardinal Hideaway. How can I help you?"

The handsome man gave me a kind smile. "I believe my fiance was just in here. She's about my height. Dark blond hair in a high ponytail. Black leather jacket."

I nodded and pointed toward the now partially open doors to the Reading Room. "She went in there."

"Thank you so much." With a grin, he headed off in that direction.

As desperate as I was to walk over and eavesdrop on the conversation happening, I knew it was unprofessional and unethical. Related to Lukas or not, that was not something you did to guests. Everyone deserved their privacy. *Besides, Quinn will tell me later, right?*

I was literally saved by the bell when a call came in, and by the time I wrapped it up, Quinn and the blond man were walking out of the Reading Room.

"Should I be concerned? We need that room in an hour."

He pulled the door shut, then patted her arm. "Don't worry, Auntie Kin. Their fights can get intense and scary as hell, but they don't last long. Give them ten, maybe fifteen minutes. They'll either sort it out or wear themselves out. Either way, it will be fine."

What did I miss during that phone call? And Auntie Kin? How is Quinn an aunt, and how did I miss that?

Quinn glanced over at Connor, who was still sitting in his chair. He nodded at her and went back to reading.

The two of them walked to the front desk, where I was desperately trying to keep a neutral, professional face on. "Everything okay?"

Quinn nodded. "Oh yeah. As it turns out, Lukas has a brother *and* a sister."

I glanced at the still-closed door. "And that was the sister?"

Quinn nodded again. "And this is Ben. He's my nephew."

What? My attention bounced back and forth between her face and Ben's. "You... you have a younger sister though... and he's... He looks her age. How?"

Ben started laughing and glanced at Quinn. "You love that intro, don't you?"

She shrugged. "Don't you? It's hilarious to watch people try to figure out the math." Turning to me, "Did you forget about my other sister Evie? She's only a year younger than me, and you forget, I'm older than I look."

I shook my head. "I didn't forget her... but you have nieces... and they are little." As I trailed off, I looked Ben up and down. "And you're all grown up."

"Ben and his younger brother were older when they were adopted by Evie's best friends. Those best friends have been part of my family, and when Ben became part of theirs, I became his aunt."

Hold on a second. "So, you two aren't actually related... like biologically?"

"Nope, but I still keep her around." Ben elbowed Quinn playfully, then turned back toward me. "Unique family tree aside, I have an actual lodge-related question for you."

Shit. I'm at work. Pull it together, Chels. "Oh. Right. Of course. How can I help you?"

"Lianne and I are going to be here for a few days, and we were hoping to stay in one of the cabins while we're here."

I scrunched up my eyebrows as I checked the computer. *Shit.* "Oh, dear. All the cabins are booked up for the next two weeks. But... Well... Maybe I can figure something out." I started clicking around to see if we could possibly upgrade one of the cabin reservations to a suite.

"What are we figuring out?" Lianne was striding toward us from the direction of the Reading Room.

I smiled at her. "I was just telling your fiance here that there weren't any cabins, but if I made some calls..."

Lianne waved her hands at me. "Please don't feel you owe me anything because my brother happens to be a whiz with a paintbrush and that your coworker is dating him. We'll happily take an available room in the lodge and will make sure to call ahead and reserve a cabin for the next time we come out."

"You can always use my cabin. I can clean it up and stay in the lodge for a couple of nights. I'm sure Frank won't mind."

She shot Quinn an annoyed look. "Quinn, I am not going to kick you out of your home. Wait, did you say Frank? How do you know him?"

"Yeah, he's my boss, one of the owners, and Edith's husband."

Lianne leaned forward onto the front desk, her shoulders shaking from laughter. "Oh, this is amazing."

Quinn looked over at Ben, who was shaking his head. "Lianne's cat's name is Frank."

Ooh! I couldn't help but giggle a little.

Lianne stood up again, taking a deep breath to regain her composure before looking at me. "I'm sorry. I didn't mean to be rude, but the mental image of my cat approving lodging choices was too funny. That aside, while I appreciate you offering up your cabin, Ben and I will happily stay in the lodge this time. Besides, we've heard a lot about Edith's baking and cooking, and we want to be as close to it as possible." She leaned forward and dropped her voice to a whisper. "Honestly, I think Ben's looking forward to her baking more than being on a mini vacation with me."

Ben blushed adorably. "That's not true. Amazing baked goods are just icing on the cake."

Quinn patted him on the shoulder. "It's totally worth the hype. I've had to up my exercise routine since working here to make sure I don't have to buy an entire new wardrobe."

Lianne turned to me again. "So, what room options are available to us?"

I had a little over an hour before the check-in rush started, and I was taking advantage of the momentary lull to put up a few more decorations.

I had just finished adding to the fireplace mantle decor when Connor suddenly stood up and headed toward the main entrance. He didn't leave, but just stood there, staring out, like he was waiting for something.

Almost immediately, Phil and Ryan walked in, and the men exchanged a tense look before Ryan headed in the direction of Quinn's office.

After Connor walked toward the elevator, I hurried over to Phil. "Is something going on?"

He glanced in the direction Ryan had headed and then over his shoulder. "Yes, and no. I'm going to be in the lobby for now."

My response was cut off by Quinn's quiet protesting.

"I don't understand why I can't just stay locked in my office with one of you guys."

Ryan let out a deep sigh. "It's not that simple right now."

Like it had been planned, the elevator door opened, and Connor gestured to it. "Come on, Quinn, we're going up to see Lianne."

My fiery co-worker glared at him. "And *then* will you tell me what in the hell is going on?"

"Yes."

"Good. You'd better."

The elevator doors closed, and I was left standing in the middle of the foyer, stunned. Ryan somehow managed to leave as quickly as he had shown up, and before I knew it, Phil was standing in front of me.

"It's going to be okay, Chelsea."

I shot him a skeptical look. "Is it?"

He nodded curtly before checking his phone again. "I'm going to personally make sure of it."

With a shake of my head, I headed back to the front desk, desperately trying to pretend this secret service crap was an everyday occurrence. I had almost convinced myself nothing was happening until I heard a muffled bang. *What in the hell was that?*

I glanced over at Phil, who locked eyes with me and then headed toward the hallway Quinn's office was in. "Hey, where are you going?"

His jaw tensed. "I need to check something."

"But you said yo—"

"I've got Chelsea and the main entrance. Go."

Peter's voice startled me, and I jumped a little, turning my attention to him. "Was that a gunshot?"

"I think a car just backfired."

Right. I arched an eyebrow and shook my head. "*Of course* it did. Because we have *so* many cars parked in the back of the lodge." He opened his mouth, but I waved him off. "I promise to tell any guests that groundskeeping was doing some maintenance on one of their larger pieces of equipment and the engine backfired. I don't want chaos and pandemonium here anymore than the next person."

"Thank you." Peter gave me a grateful smile and returned to his surveillance of the main entrance and parking lot. He glanced at his phone a minute later and shook his head.

"Everything good up here, Chelsea?"

I looked up at the kind dark brown eyes of Borce. "Hey. I'm fine, just waiting for the check in crowd to show. Busy afternoon in *your* department, though, huh?"

He nodded and let out a tense chuckle. "You could say that. Miles and I are going to help out with check-in today. I'll be in here, and he'll be out helping unload and bring in luggage."

"That's not standard protocol. If everything is okay, why all the extra people up front?"

The older man took a deep breath and let it out slowly. "Today hasn't been standard, Chelsea. And while things are better at the moment, we're just being cautious right now."

A quick glance around showed me Peter was now gone and Miles was already staging the luggage carts.

"Well, it's a lighter day with the art festival being over, but I appreciate the help all the same."

I was in the middle of checking in a guest when movement near the Reading Room caught my eye. Peter and Lukas walked in and headed in the direction of the security office. *Well, at least Lukas is okay.*

I had just finished checking in my third guest of the afternoon when I clocked Lukas heading toward the elevator, probably to see Quinn. It only took the time of one more check-in to pass before I saw Peter appear in the corner of the foyer just before Quinn burst out of the elevator, frustration all over her face. She immediately bee-lined toward and out the back door, with Peter a respectful distance behind her.

She was barely outside when Lukas and Connor popped out of the stairwell door as well. When he glanced at me, I pointed toward the Reading Room and back door, mouthing the word "outside." Both men gave me a grateful look and headed out.

Looks like someone is in the doghouse with Quinn. That ought to make things even more interesting around here.

Chapter Three

Chelsea

The days following the half-lockdown were just as chaotic, but for business reasons. Lukas's sister decided she wanted her wedding at the lodge, and soon. The following week, to be exact. After I found out the woman was obsessed with all things Christmas, I wanted to make sure the lobby, and lodge in general, had as many of the wonderful decorations and trimmings as possible.

I'd already made a phone call to Chuck's Nursery and Tree Farm to get the tree for the lobby and had Chuck, the owner and a personal friend, make sure it was delivered and set up ASAP. I wanted it to be perfect. I also ordered a few wreaths to hang in different areas of the foyer and outside entrance area.

Peter was in the foyer the morning the tree was delivered and was kind enough to help me and Lynn decorate, and by decorate, I meant he pulled boxes out of the conference room and made sure we didn't fall off chairs and ladders. We all wanted the trees up and fully decorated ASAP in case Quinn needed any extra help pulling together things for Lianne and Ben's wedding.

That afternoon I was absolutely giddy, bouncing, twirling, and humming Christmas carols while putting the finishing touches on everything in the lobby. This was my absolute favorite time of year, and I ate up every single moment of it. As I took in both of the completely decorated trees, as well as the hearth, it felt like the holiday season was truly upon us.

A snicker startled me and I spun around. "Oh, hi, Quinn. How long have you been standing there?"

My favorite new co-worker walked toward me, a wide grin on her face. "Long enough to hear and see an extremely amusing rendition of 'Jingle Bell Rock' with the most glorious choreography. I think what impressed me the most was how you also managed to finish decorating the front desk at the same time."

"Not the first time I've decorated this lobby." I glanced around, taking in my handiwork. The entire reception desk was draped with evergreen garland and white twinkle lights. I still wanted to add some more glitz, but that was something I could add later. I knew I could decorate the lobby the same way every year, but that was boring and lacked all creativity. Frank and Edith didn't mind that I fussed over their lobby. They loved that I took so much pride in making the entire foyer festive.

"I know you're our personal bundle of holiday cheer, but you seem to be in an extra good mood today."

I smiled at Quinn. "I'm going to pick out my tree this weekend."

The excited expression dropped from her face and was immediately replaced with anxiety and fear. "You're not going alone, are you?"

"Quinn, we've been through this, remember? Phil said he'd go with me, but if he's busy, I'll be fine. No one is going to mess with me while I go pick out and chop down a Christmas tree. And as a reminder, no one has made sure I get to and from work or the bar or June's house, and nothing has happened. I'm pretty insignificant in the grand scheme of things."

Quinn's jaw clenched as she took a deep breath. "That was

before... You're not..." She trailed off and shook her head. "Please make sure Phil or Peter can go with you." Her slightly tearful blue eyes bored into mine, pleading with me.

I wanted to argue the point with her. I wanted to push back. I wanted to be insulted, but the fear in her eyes stopped me cold in my tracks. It felt a bit of an overreaction, but this was not the time to call her out. *She's really worried about this. What happened?* I knew her ex was doubling down with his ridiculous games, but right now I was worried more about her than me. That woman was stubborn and independent, but not always to her personal benefit.

It was about this time that Phil walked around the corner. He looked between me and Quinn and rushed over. "Is everything okay?"

Quinn swallowed and nodded, immediately putting on her cheerful customer service face. "Everything is fine."

Phil stared at Quinn and arched an eyebrow. "You sure about that? It would be a whole lot more convincing if you hadn't wiped a tear away first."

I rolled my eyes and shook my head. "What my dear friend and coworker isn't saying is that she was freaking out at the thought of me going out and collecting a Christmas tree without one of you fine gentlemen joining me."

He glanced at me, toward Quinn, and then back at me, brow furrowed in confusion. "I already said I'd be happy to join you."

My heart fluttered at his offer and it took some effort not to show how happy it made me. "I know, but I wouldn't want to inconvenience you. You have far more important things to do than following me halfway up a mountain to cut a tree down."

Phil shrugged. "While I'm working, sure, but I don't work all day, every day. I do have time off. Let me know when you want to go, and I'll make sure I'll be able to join you. Wait, did you say a tree farm?"

I turned to face Phil. "Yeah. Why?"

"I'm just a little surprised you're going to a tree farm."

"Why?"

He shrugged and then pulled his phone out of his pocket, frowning a little as he stared at the screen. "Just surprised you weren't buying a precut one, that's all. Lukas needs me. I'll be back around later." He nodded at each of us, winking at me. "Ladies."

I didn't realize Quinn had been watching me watch Phil walk away until the phone rang and I ran into her when I turned to walk back to the desk.

"I can't wait to hear about how your Christmas tree date goes." And before I could respond, she turned on her heel and walked away, leaving me flustered and having to deal with the ringing phone.

Phil

Quinn: < btw - I gave Chelsea your number to facilitate scheduling the tree outing. I'm attaching her contact info as well. >

I couldn't stop the smile that appeared on my face.

Phil: < Thanks. Does she know? >

Quinn. < Yeah, I just told her. >

Quinn: < And thank you, again. It makes me feel so better knowing she's got back up if she needs it, especially with how Justin has been MIA since... you know. >

The guys and I had found it more than suspicious that after Ryan pulled the in-depth background check, Justin called off sick the next two days he had to work. Even more suspicious? The address he put on his paperwork, while a legitimate address, was that of his aunt and not where he actually lived. She didn't even know he was back in town. All of which were more red flags, but somewhat useless ones at this point. We'd already figured out he was bad news.

Phil: < Not a problem at all. I want to keep everyone here safe and in one piece as much as you do. >

I took a deep breath as I settled against the headboard of my bed, added Chelsea's contact info to my phone, and sent her a message.

Phil: < Hey, it's Phil. Let me know what time you want to head out to get your Christmas tree. >

Phil: < I'm good any time after 2pm. (Working the overnight.) Where do you want to meet? >

Chelsea: < How about 2:30 at my house? Or we can meet at the lodge. >

Phil: < I'm fine meeting at your place. >

She sent me her address, and I added it to her info.

"What's got you smiling over there?"

I shook my head at Peter, who sat on his bed in our shared lodge room. "Just doing Quinn a favor, and she's being overly grateful."

Peter chuckled. "Would that favor have anything to do with the gorgeous blond behind the front desk?"

I wanted to be pissed that he'd called her gorgeous, but even a blind man would have figured out how beautiful she was. "Yeah. Quinn asked me. She wants me to make sure Chelsea gets her Christmas tree without harassment. I think the entire Justin situation, combined with Jeffery's *gift* from the other day, has rattled her more than she's willing to admit."

"She's got a right to be rattled. Though, I have to admit she's taking this way better than most people I've seen in similar situations."

I glanced up from my phone. "Quinn might act like a tough cookie, but she's struggling. She's really good at putting on a professional happy face, but she's battling some major demons under the surface."

Peter nodded. "I've noticed that, too, and so has Connor."

"I like her. She's good for Lukas, and he's good for her."

"Kind of like you and Chelsea?"

I froze for a moment. "What are you talking about?"

"Listen, I know you're probably going to say something about how you're just doing your job and being friendly, but I've seen how you two look at each other." Peter shifted on the couch and stared at me. "No judgment. There's nothing that says you can't be with her. While she is an employee of the lodge, and *technically* under our care, she isn't specifically assigned to us for a security detail. You're free to pursue her if that's what you want. All I'm saying is to proceed with caution, man. You know the potential perils of mixing work and play."

Tell me something I haven't already thought to death. "Yeah, yeah, yeah. I know. I'm just making sure she finds a tree and gets home unharassed."

My friend chuckled, clearly not believing me. "Does that include harassment from you?"

A smirk tugged at the corner of my mouth. "It's not harassment if she wants it."

He arched an eyebrow. "Careful how you say that, Phil. You're a short step from sounding like one of those misogynistic assholes."

I glared at him. "I'm not like that, and you know it."

Chapter Four

Phil

When I walked into the lobby Friday night, I was surprised how much more decorated it was than twenty-four hours ago. The entrances to the Reading Room were draped with light-wrapped evergreen garland, and all the other doors in sight had evergreen swags with gold and silver sparkly bows on them. *Did Chelsea do all this in a day?*

"Hey, Phillip. Impressed?"

I glanced over at Damien, the night desk guy, and nodded. "This looks amazing."

He sighed as he looked around the space. "Chelsea really knocked it out of the park this year. I mean, she always does, but this may be her best work yet. I think Quinn *might* have something to do with it as well. Those two women can be intimidating as hell and an absolute force when they team up and tackle something."

"No arguments there." Damien wasn't wrong.

Much to my delight, my night was quiet and eventless. There was nothing out of the ordinary when I checked the cameras and walked the building inside and out. And while it was a relief to have nothing happen, the peace almost put me on edge.

Toward the end of my shift, after writing down a few notes for Peter and leaving them in the security office, I headed into the kitchen and started a pot of coffee. I knew I'd be going to bed soon, but I'd come to enjoy sharing a mug with Edith while she cooked me some breakfast. The day she found out I usually only ate a protein bar before going to bed, I thought she was going to reprimand Lukas and put him in the corner for not taking care of his employees. From that day on, it was standard protocol for anyone working overnight to stop by the kitchen and have breakfast before going to bed. I made it a point to try to have the coffee started so it was one last thing she had to worry about.

I was pouring myself a mug of coffee when Edith walked in.

"I'm surprised you need caffeine with all the excitement happening later on today."

"What excitement?" I added a spoonful of sugar and handed the mug to her.

She arched an eyebrow and grinned as she took a sip of her coffee. "Don't play coy with me young man. I know you're going out with our Chelsea later on today."

I nodded. "Yeah. Quinn asked me to keep an eye on her."

"Right. *That's* the reason you're going." She set the mug down and walked toward the fridge. "Scrambled eggs, bacon, and toast sound good?"

I am never going to hear the end of this, am I? I tried my best to move past the conversation topic. "That sounds delicious."

By the time Edith finished making breakfast, and I finished eating it, the tired settled in and I found myself starting to drift off.

"Off to bed now. You need to get all that beauty sleep in before your big outing later."

Grinning and shaking my head, I headed out, only staying awake long enough to set my alarm once I was in my room.

A thunk from the hallway startled me from my sleep. It sounded like one of the housekeeping carts bumping into the wall. After taking a deep breath, I blinked several times, clearing the sleep from my eyes. *What time is it?* Rolling over, I grabbed my phone and saw it was 12:15 pm. I had a little over an hour to get ready and head out.

After I was out of the shower, dressed, and put on my shoes, there was a knock on the door. A smirk slid onto my face when I saw Quinn through the peephole, standing there fidgeting. I unlocked the door and opened it. "Hey, what's up?"

Her eyes lit up and relief washed over her face when she saw me. "Oh, good. You're awake. I just wanted to make sure."

I gave her a gentle smile, fully understanding why she was so on edge about this. "I'm a man of my word, Quinn. I know how important this is to you."

"I know... I'm just..." She trailed off.

I stepped forward and put my hand on her shoulder. "I get it. and please believe me when I say you're not overreacting. You're taking this seriously, and I appreciate that you're not fighting us on keeping you safe."

Quinn let out a tense breath and leaned against the door jamb. "You really don't think I'm overreacting?"

"Nope. We've seen some of what Jeffery, and possibly Justin, are capable of. You wouldn't be the only one who'd feel guilty if something happened to Chelsea. And for what it's worth, we've also made sure she gets home okay and have been keeping an eye on her place."

She nodded, took a deep breath, and let it out slowly. "I appreciate it. Also, she's already here. It's part of the reason I came and knocked on your door."

Interesting. "Thanks for letting me know. I'll be right out."

Quinn chuckled. "I'll leave you to it, then. Have fun."

In record time I finished getting ready and headed out to the lobby, shaking my head when I spotted Chelsea in the Reading Room, measuring the window widths. "I thought I was picking you up?"

She turned and smiled sheepishly at me. "You were, but I wanted to grab a few measurements. I couldn't remember the width of our standard guest room door."

"I could have measured it for you."

Chelsea shrugged. "I didn't want to inconvenience you."

A chuckle came out. "You thought asking me to measure the width of the door I walk through multiple times a day would be an inconvenience?"

She chewed on her bottom lip, which was adorable. "It sounds a little silly when you say it like that."

I took the measuring tape from her hands, walked back to my door, measured it, and walked back to her. "The door is thirty-six inches wide and with the casing is forty inches. Need anything else measured?"

The pink that appeared on Chelsea's cheeks as she shook her head 'no' told me she caught the subtle innuendo I'd dropped.

"Shall we head out?"

Chelsea

The wide-eyed look on Phil's face when I popped my small chainsaw and handsaw into the back of his truck was going to live in my head forever. It was obvious the man was used to being the muscle and hero of the day, but that ego needed to be checked.

I hurried to get into the passenger's seat before Phil made his way to the driver's side. I needed a few seconds to pull myself together. It was one thing to flirt playfully with him while I was at work, but now we were going to be together... alone... and for at least a couple hours. It was everything I wanted, but now that it was here and actually happening, I was nervous and a little on edge.

Come on, Chels. Pull yourself together.

The ride to the tree farm was relatively quiet, which only made me feel more nervous, though I was desperately trying to play it cool. Eventually my resolve broke, and I reached over to turn on the radio, putting on some Christmas music. I needed comfort and distraction and was surprised by the lack of reaction from him.

When I started singing along to the radio, I couldn't help but notice the little smile that appeared on his face.

We were in the parking lot twenty minutes later, and I was out of the truck retrieving my tools from the back. Phil, to no one's surprise, was right behind me as I walked through the entrance.

"Heya, Chelsea! I wondered if I was going to be seeing you this weekend."

A wide grin spread across my face as I went to hug one of my dear friends I'd grown up with. "Hey, Chuck! You know I still need to get the best Christmas tree for my house."

He chuckled and then glanced behind me. "Brought extra muscle this year, I see. Planning on upgrading to a larger tree?"

I laughed as I glanced over my shoulder and winked at Phil. "Something like that. I have my heart set on a Douglas Fir this year. I know I got a Colorado Blue Spruce last year, but I really like the look of that Douglas fir that Frank and Edith have in the lobby."

Chuck nodded. "It's a beauty. How tall of a tree are you looking for?"

"At least six feet. I want to feel dwarfed by it."

He shook his head as he chuckled again. "Head off along path three. You'll want to walk farther down to get a tree that hasn't been manhandled by everyone."

"Of course." I glanced over my shoulder again and looked at the hottie Quinn had begged me to bring along. *Why did I fight this?* A delightfully playful idea popped into my head. "Ready to go hug a tree or two?"

Phil shot me a confused and amused look. "I thought we were cutting one?"

"Well, yeah, but you have to find the perfect one first."

"And this involved hugging them?"

I giggled, ignoring the coughed over snicker from behind me. "Yep. Gotta make sure those branches are both strong and pliable." *Is he going to buy this? Can I actually get him to hug a tree? That would be the best Christmas present ever!*

Phil studied me for a moment and then let out a sigh. "Lead the way, Miss Lumberjack."

Chuck shook his head at me as I waved at him and headed into the rows of trees. *This is going to be the best day ever!*

Phil

Chelsea was a terrible liar, and her friend running the tree farm wasn't exactly hiding his amused reaction to her story. I knew the tree hugging thing was a load of crap. Was I going to call her out? Not a chance. The way her eyes sparkled and the laughter that bubbled out of her made my heart race, and I was willing to do just about anything to maintain that level of joy. Like apparently follow her through a Christmas tree farm and carry her handsaw and chainsaw while dragging a modified sled.

Carrying her tools wasn't really a hardship, and following that tiny, curvy goddess was a privilege and honor. Seeing Chelsea outside of work in those jeans that fit her perfectly made me want to pull her toward me and learn every inch of her.

Focus.

"What do you think of this one?"

I glanced at the tree she gestured to. "It looks nice, though I'm not entirely sure what your perfect tree looks like."

"You need to hug it."

"What?"

Chelsea put her hands on her hips, standing there with a wide grin on her face. "You heard me. I need you to hug this tree."

"It's not going to prove anything."

"If you're afraid of getting poked, just say it."

Not so gently tossing the rope to the sled at her, I headed toward the tree. "I prefer to be the one doing the poking." I wrapped my arms around part of the tree, being mindful not to damage any of the branches in case this was the tree she wanted. "Yeah, this feels like a good one." I shook my head, feeling mildly like an idiot for doing this. The absolute look of delight on her face had me grinning. "You might want to double-check my findings, though." I winked at her.

Chelsea chuckled. "No, I believe you. I think I found a better tree."

I followed her gaze to a slightly taller, fuller tree a little farther down the row. "That one looks really nice."

She walked toward it, taking a slow lap around it. After a moment, Chelsea's entire face lit up. "It's perfect."

"Yeah, it is." But I wasn't looking at the tree. I was looking at her and trying to think of all the reasons why it would be a bad idea to back her into another tree and kiss the breath out of her. The only one I could come up with was that she was sort of my co-worker, and I didn't know if there was a policy about dating coworkers. The last thing I wanted to do was cause her problems at work. I inwardly yelled at myself for being a coward.

"Yep. She's perfect. Time to take her down and bring her home." Chelsea walked over to the sled and grabbed both of her saws. I nearly had to restrain myself when she bent over to check something at the base of the trunk, that perfect behind pointed in my direction. Suddenly, she stood up and glanced over. "Want to be helpful?"

"Always. What do you need?"

"Can you spot the other side and redirect the tree to make sure it doesn't hit any of the other trees and break any branches? I'm going to do my best from my end, and while I'm good at this, I'm not an expert."

I moved to the other side of the tree, and while she had cut the trunk in such a way to aim it away from everything else, I still had to do a minor redirect.

Chelsea started to pull the tree toward the sled but was having a hard time moving it.

"Here, let me help." I squatted down, looping my arm around several of the bottom branches, and with very little effort dragged the tree to its chariot out of here. "I guess it was a good thing you brought along a little extra muscle this year."

She snickered and rolled her eyes. "Yeah, yeah, yeah. Don't let it go to your head."

I gestured toward the now-loaded sled. "You're welcome to pull it."

"And deny myself the pleasure of watching you and your muscles? Nah. *That* part of your ego, I'm all about seeing."

Chelsea

It wasn't a hardship watching Phil maneuver the tree onto the sled and help me bring it up to the checkout area. I could watch him lift and carry things all day. Shaking the thought from my head, I surged forward and put some distance between us before I embraced the urge to throw myself at him and kiss the hell out of him. *He's not here to make out with me. He's here to make sure Quinn's ex or one of his idiot friends doesn't do something stupid. Nothing else.*

Chuck gave me a playful smirk when I walked up. "Find everything you were looking for?"

And then some. I chuckled. "Well, I found the perfect tree."

He nodded. "Excellent. That's what I like to hear."

By the time I finished paying for it, Chuck's employee had wrapped the tree and Phil waited for me.

"You could have headed off to the truck. You didn't have to wait for me."

Phil arched an eyebrow and stared at me. "Wouldn't that kind of defeat a major purpose of my presence?"

A major purpose? Why else would he have wanted to come with me? "I suppose." I narrowed my eyes as I studied him, trying not to smile figure out what other motive he might have had.

Securing the tree to the top of the trick took almost no time at all, and before I realized it, we were heading out and on our way to my house. I couldn't help the sadness that settled over me. Even hearing my favorite Christmas song on the radio didn't put a full smile on my face. I didn't want our time together to end.

I kept glancing over and stealing glimpses of Phil. He hadn't shaved before coming with, and the scruff had been a distraction. *Who knew I liked a little facial hair?*

"Would you like help getting this beauty inside?" His eyes twinkled with mischief as he asked the question.

"Which beauty?"

A wide smile appeared on his face. "Either."

I loved this banter with him, but still wondered if he wanted to be here. Would he have come if Quinn hadn't asked? "You're more than welcome to take both of us inside."

"Don't mind if I do." I swear his cheeks pinked up slightly before he opened the truck door and hopped out. *Good. I don't want to be the only flustered one here.*

Phil carried in the tree like it weighed nothing and we had it set up in its stand in no time. Once the netting came off, he was on the ground with my handsaw, trimming a few of the lower branches, making sure it fit perfectly in my living room.

I stood there just staring at it when he stood up and walked over.

"Do you have any heavy-duty string?"

I tipped my head to the side. "I do. Why?"

Phil shrugged. "I could make a wreath for you out of the pieces I just trimmed off."

What? "No way!"

A grin spread across his face. "Yes, way."

I ran to the kitchen and pulled a ball of twine out of my junk drawer. "Will this work?"

He nodded. "Perfect."

While he sat at my kitchen table and fussed with the extra branches, I opened up the closet under the stairs and brought out several totes full of lights, ornaments, and other decorations.

His eyes were wide when I walked past him and brought in two more totes from the small storage unit just off my back patio. "Are those your Christmas decorations?"

I shook my head. "Not all of it, no. This is just for the tree and main level."

"There's more?"

A chuckle bubbled out of me. "Yes, there's more. I have upstairs decorations and outdoor decorations, too."

Phil nodded as he took in the stack of totes. "Any ribbon in there I can use?"

"What do you need ribbon for?"

He shook his head and smirked at me. "I'm making something,

and I want it to look nice."

"Okay." The most amazing, warm feeling filled my chest, as I went digging for a spool of gold ribbon I knew I had. Leaving it on the table, I went about distracting myself from what he was doing by unpacking the strings of lights and testing to see if they still worked.

By the time I started to string the lights up, Phil had rejoined me in the living room. I hated to admit it but having a taller person helping me made it go so much faster. When the tree was lit, I stood back to admire it.

"Want to see something else that might also put a smile on your face?"

I nodded, and he led me over to the kitchen table. On it was one of the most beautiful wreaths I'd ever seen. He'd twisted the branches in such a way I couldn't tell where one branch started and the other ended. The gold ribbon was wrapped criss-cross around the entire thing, with an intricate bow on the bottom. *How did he make that?* "Phil! This is amazing!" I turned to face him and wrapped him in the biggest hug. "Thank you."

It took a second for him to hug me back, but then we stood there for a lot longer than any standard issue hug.

No complaints here.

His phone went off, regrettably ending the hug. After reading whatever was on the screen, he let out a sigh. "I gotta head back. You want to tag along so you can pick up your car, or do you want one of us to bring it back here for you?"

My car! "I completely forgot about it still being at the lodge." I looked around, taking in the decorations strewn about the living room. "Would it be a huge pain in the butt for someone to bring it over later? Like whenever you're all not busy? I have every inten- tion of spending the next day and a half here."

"I wouldn't have offered if I didn't want to do that for you."

"Oh. Well, thank you. I appreciate it."

He stepped closer to me, tucking a loose hair behind my ear. "I had fun today."

"Me too." The words came out as a whisper.

We stood, my heart racing as we started into each other's eyes. With how his hand trembled, I knew he was feeling something, too, and then his phone buzzed again.

Phil sighed and glanced at his phone screen, his lips pressing into a tight line as he read whatever. "I'll let you know when I'm bringing your car back." He gave me one more hug, kissed the top of my head, and headed out.

I wistfully watched out my front window as he pulled out of the driveway and drove away. For as much as I'd fought against having him here in the first place, now I was sad he'd left. Twenty minutes later, my phone went off.

Quinn: < I see you and Phil had a good time today. >

I furrowed my brows in confusion. *What did she see?*

Quinn: < There was a huge grin on his face when he walked in a few minutes ago. One that got bigger when I asked how his day went. ;) >

Quinn: < I look forward to our Monday morning chat and hearing your gratitude and how I was right. >

I bet she is. I shook my head at her antics, then glanced at the gorgeous wreath sitting on my coffee table, and grinned. Phil had done such an amazing job, and while I wanted nothing more than to hang it on my front door for everyone to see, I also wanted it inside so I could see it all the time.

Without another thought, I stood up, grabbed my power drill from the kitchen, sank a screw into the wall behind the door, and hung the wreath. I'd be able to see it from the couch and pass it every time I went upstairs. *Perfect.*

Chapter Five

Phil

I was eternally grateful that Peter wasn't in the room when I got back from Chelsea's. I wanted to sit and take a minute without getting grilled about today or the reason I couldn't stop smiling. Quinn had only asked how my day went, and while the look in her eye told me there was a lot more she wanted to know, I didn't get interrogated.

Peter had known where I was going, and he knew I liked her, but that didn't mean I wanted to hear all about it. The razzing was unavoidable, but I could at least put it off for a few hours. *Well, until after this meeting with Ryan.* He'd texted me while I was with Chelsea, and now I needed to meet up with him.

I was about to head to the security office when my phone went off.

Chelsea: < Found the perfect spot! >

Attached was a picture of the wreath I'd made her hanging up on the wall behind the front door.

Chelsea: < Now I can see it more than when I leave or come home. >

She wants to see it all the time? She must have really liked it. The picture and the thought put a smile on my face.

"Someone had a good day."

I let out a slightly annoyed sigh as Peter walked into the room. *Here it comes.* "I did. How was yours?"

He flopped onto his bed and stared at me. "Pretty quiet here, all things considered. It couldn't have been better than traipsing around with some gorgeous bombshell."

"I wasn't *traipsing around.* I was keeping her safe at Quinn's request."

Peter shot me a pointed stare. "Sure, Phil. Whatever you say. You ready to head over to chat with Ryan?"

"Yeah. Do you know what it's about?"

He shrugged. "I don't think it's an emergency, whatever it is, but his text still seemed urgent. My gut is telling me he's extra worked up about Lianne and Ben's wedding."

It wasn't too far from the thoughts I was having about it. "That wouldn't surprise me. Maybe it's about how we are going to cover things?"

"Maybe."

I nodded. "Let me reply to this, see if Edith has any coffee, and I'll be right there."

Peter chuckled as he headed toward the door. "You know she keeps an extra pot on at all times for us, right?"

Phil: < It looks perfect on that wall. What's next on the decorating list tonight? >

Chelsea: < The tree. Duh. ;). >

Phil: < I can't wait to see how you decorate it. >

Chelsea: < I'll make sure to take pictures. >

Phil: < Maybe I'll even decorate something. You've inspired me. >

Chelsea: < Now THIS I'm going to have to see. >

. . .

With a smile on my face, I headed out of my room and to the kitchen. After Edith found out I was heading into a meeting, she packed up a basket with cookies and muffins, two carafes of coffee, and enough mugs for all of us.

Ryan smiled when we walked into his room bearing gifts. "I see you made a pit stop on the way here."

I smiled and nodded. "I was just going to grab a cup of coffee, but as you can see, Edith happened."

He crossed the room and opened the basket as soon as I set it on the small table next to the couch. "Yes! She sent muffins." Without hesitation, Ryan bit into one of the blueberry muffins and let out a small, pleased groan. "I'm going to miss these once we're done here."

I shook my head and filled a mug with coffee and a splash of cream before sitting on the couch. "Is Connor staying with Quinn while we're here?" I knew there was no way Lukas was going to let Quinn be unchaperoned for a second until this was resolved.

Ryan shook his head. "No. Quinn is going to be with Ben and Lianne so we all can be here."

As if on cue, there was a knock on the door right before it opened and Lukas and Connor walked in, both of them looking a little more tense than usual.

That's never good. "Everything okay?"

Lukas nodded as he headed to the basket to grab a cookie and fill a mug with coffee. "As good as it can be at the moment."

I glanced at Peter, who shrugged, and then at Ryan, who raised an eyebrow, silently asking for more information.

Connor pressed his lips into a straight line before commenting. "We've lost track of both Jeffery and Justin. It's like they just vanished."

"What? How?" This wasn't good.

Lukas let out a deep sigh. "That's what we've been trying to figure out."

"No one can disappear like that, not unless they know *exactly* what they are doing." Connor now sat on the edge of the bed, his elbows resting on his knees. "They've got really good connections. Our expertise level of connections. I don't like it. At all."

"None of us do." Ryan was back to sitting in his desk chair, gently swaying side to side.

Lukas nodded. "It's been way too quiet since Jeffery sent his minion with that *present* for Quinn. My contact hasn't seen or heard anything, either. It's too good to be true. Something is coming, and I feel like a sitting duck." He glanced over at me. "Did you notice anything when you were out with Chelsea?"

I shook my head. "We weren't in town, and the few people we interacted with seemed on the up and up."

A smirk tugged at the corner of his mouth for a moment before he nodded. "Good to hear, even if it doesn't make me feel any better about the situation."

There was a moment of strained silence, and the frustration of not being on top of the situation was palpable in the room.

"So, what's the plan for the wedding, and are we going to have a bigger meeting with your dad and brother, too?"

I smiled at Peter, grateful he directed us back to something we had control over.

"In her words? 'I want people I trust wholly keeping us safe.' So, no pressure, guys." Letting out a sigh, Lukas dove into the plan.

After a long meeting with Lukas and the team and another long video meeting with Mr. Agosti and Gage, we were all as ready as we could be for the night. Borce, who joined us during the video call, told everyone to take the night off. When Mr. Agosti agreed, there was no arguing.

"I know how hard you boys work. I also trust Borce to hold down the fort for one night without you lot breathing down his neck. If he needs you, he knows where you are and how to reach you."

Not wanting to get in trouble, we ended the meeting and headed off in separate directions. Lukas veered off to see Quinn, Ryan went to his room, and on the way back to ours, Peter let me know he wanted to watch a movie.

"I'm going to spend some time in the Reading Room in front of that fireplace."

It didn't take long for me to change into pajamas, grab my book, and head out. I was halfway through my post-apocalyptic book about created shifters and clones trying to keep their small town alive, fed, and safe. The guys could have their action and war movies and documentaries. I liked my books to have happy endings.

"You need anything, hun?"

I glanced up and smiled at Edith. Her coat was draped over her arm, and she had her free hand on her hip.

"No, I'm good. I appreciate you checking in, though."

She grinned. "Did you have a good time with Chelsea today?"

"I did. She knows how to pick the perfect tree. I see you're heading out. Do you need me to head back to my room?"

"No, sweetie. You're welcome to stay in here as long as you want. I trust you not to burn down my lovely lodge."

A smirk tugged at the corner of my lips. "I wouldn't dare."

Once she left, closing the doors behind her, my attention drifted back to the fireplace. I let myself get lost in the flicker and dance of the flames. As I watched the mesmerizing show of the fire, I thought again about Chelsea and her excitement about the holiday. Her cheer and spirit were infectious as well as addicting.

I spent more time fighting the urge to go get another dose of her personality than I did thinking about anything else. It had been a long time since I felt that drawn to anyone. Lecturing myself about keeping my cool and not wildly jumping in with both feet, I wasn't sure how much time had passed, and was only brought out of my thoughts by the buzzing of my phone.

Chelsea: < Everything okay over there? Quinn mentioned something about a testosterone fueled meeting earlier. >

I snickered and shook my head. *Of course, Quinn told her about the meeting.*

Phil: < Nothing to worry about. Just us making plans for this week and all the festivities and extra people. >

Phil: < How's the decorating going? >

Chelsea: < The tree is looking SO GOOD! I may have outdone myself this year. >

When a picture didn't immediately pop up, I had to tease her.

Phil: < You're going to tell me it looks amazing and then not show me the final product? I see how it is. >

Chelsea: < Aren't you the impatient one? If you must know, I was taking a picture so I could send it to you, but it was taking me a second to get it just right. :-P >

A picture popped up next, and it looked like a scene you'd find on a Christmas card. The tree was wrapped in tiny white lights, dark purple ribbon, and about a million silver and white ornaments. At the top was a lit, sparkling star.

Phil: < That looks amazing! Seriously. You're really good at that. >

I pulled up the photo again and zoomed in on something to the right of the tree.

Phil: < What's the green circle thing hanging over the chair in the corner? >

Chelsea: < Mistletoe, why? >

Phil: < You need it in your house? >

I'd love to be there to take advantage of it. I shook my head to clear out the thought. Now was *not* the time to be chasing after someone. We had to get through Lianne's wedding and get to the bottom of the Jeffery crap.

Chelsea: < Would you rather it be somewhere else? Somewhere more... Accessible? >

A groan slipped out at the thought of pressing my lips to hers. This woman was testing me. *She probably knows it, too.*

Phil: < Dealer's choice. >

Chapter Six

Phil

Even though I'd dropped her car at her house and had gotten a hug, I was a little bummed about not being able to talk to Chelsea much over the next two days. Our busy schedules made that an almost impossibility. She had been working extra hours helping Quinn and Lianne prepare for the wedding, while I'd been working overtime with my team to keep the property as safe as possible and continuing the hunt for Justin and Jeffrey. That aside, I noticed mistletoe had popped up in a few places around the lodge, and I couldn't help but wonder if that was intentional. *I should take advantage of it.*

Wednesday morning rolled around, and there was less to do off-site. With an event going on in the ballroom, there was more active guard duty happening within the lodge.

I was making my rounds through the foyer when I noticed Chelsea setting up the midday cookies and hot chocolate in the Reading Room. Normally, Edith would set it up, but she was busy in the kitchen, making sure all the food was perfect for the luncheon happening in the ballroom.

When I wandered in, Chelsea was humming along to the festive music playing softly in the background. I stopped and leaned against the door jamb, not wanting to interrupt her just yet, and watched as she arranged the snacks on the table next to the window.

Suddenly, she glanced over her shoulder, smirking and shaking her head when our eyes met. "Do they just pay you to stand around and look good?"

I shrugged as I walked across the room toward her, every part of me wanting to be closer to her. "I'm making sure the room is safe and secure."

She smirked. "Is that so? And am I *safe and secure* in here?"

Finally, in front of her, I reached out and cupped her elbow, fighting the urge to pull her into my arms. "Without a doubt. Especially now since I'm here."

Chelsea rolled her eyes and snickered. "Egotistical much?"

"Is it ego if it's true?" When she shrugged, I leaned in a little. "I have a secret for you."

A grin appeared on her face, and a mischievous twinkle appeared in her eyes as she leaned a little closer to me. "What's that?"

Here goes something. I wiggled my eyebrows. "You're under mistletoe."

"What?" Chelsea glanced up and snickered at the little piece of evergreen decor above our heads. She returned her gaze to my face. "You're under it, too."

"I suppose I am." My eyes were still on hers, and I leaned in, making our faces closer than before.

"Any reason you pointed it out?" The words came out as an airy whisper.

"I think you know why." Her eyes went wide, as I wrapped my arms around her. "Breathe, Chelsea."

She gasped in a tiny breath and then swallowed hard. "Were you looking for an excuse to kiss me? Because you didn't need to come up with an elaborate plan. I've been wanting to kiss you sinc—"

I cut off her words with a kiss I'd been wanting to give her for weeks, and grinned when she melted into my arms. Her lips were softer than I'd dreamed, and I strangely loved the taste of her lip gloss more than I thought I would. The pride that surged through me as her hands gripped the side of my shirt was more energizing and potent than any cup of coffee.

This. This is everything I want.

The kiss wasn't long enough for my liking, but it had my head spinning all the same. When I pulled away, Chelsea opened her eyes, letting out the tiniest whine as she leaned toward me to extend the kiss. "We should do that again, you know, for scientific purposes."

A wide grin appeared on my face. "You want to make sure it wasn't only amazing just because it was our first kiss?"

"Something like that."

I started to lean in to kiss her again, but the phone at the front desk rang, interrupting my plan to make this moment even better.

"Shit. I have to get that. Be right back!" Chelsea tore off across the room and back into the lobby, barely catching the call. "Cardinal Hideaway. How may I help you?"

A huge breath rushed out of me as I rode the surge of emotions ranging from excited to anxious to mixed with adrenaline from the most amazing first kiss I'd ever had. I needed the phone call to be short and the day to pass quickly. There was a beautiful woman I needed to kiss again later.

Chelsea

Ten minutes later, I was still dealing with the most insufferable client on the phone. *I gave up kissing a cute guy for this?*

"I demand to speak to someone who can *actually* answer my questions."

I took a deep breath and let it out slowly. The woman on the phone was testing my patience in the worst way. "I'm sorry, ma'am, but as I told you, our Event Coordinator is in the middle of running an event at the moment. I can transfer you to her voicemail where you can leave a message, and I promise she'll get back to you as soon as she can."

There was a huff on the other end. "I'm not saying all this twice. *You* can deliver the message and have her call me back."

She's not worth getting fired over. She's not worth getting fired over. She's not worth getting fired over.

I took another deep breath and forced a smile on my face. There was no one around, and I knew she couldn't see me, but it helped me maintain my fake kindness when I was on the phone. "I'd be happy to take a message and hand it to her as soon as she's wrapped up her event."

"Glad to hear you're going to do your job, seeing as you *are* a receptionist."

I'd like to see how well you could do this job. Entitled and rude clients like this woman drove me up a wall. After making me read back my note for Quinn *and* her phone number to make sure I hadn't screwed it up, she finally ended the call. I glanced around the lobby toward the Reading Room when I saw Lynn, one of my other favorite co-workers and landscaper extraordinaire, walking in. I waved her over. "Hey, can you do me a huge favor?"

She nodded. "Sure. What's up?"

"Can you stand here for a minute while I put this note on Quinn's desk? I'd ask you to put it on her desk for me, but the rather *testy* woman this is from would probably know if I didn't do it myself, and I'd rather not incur more of her wrath."

Lynn chuckled sympathetically as she stepped behind the front desk. "Things I don't miss about working the front desk. I'll babysit the phone for you. I was looking for Frank anyway, so take a few minutes if you want. I'm in no rush."

I flashed her a grateful smile. "You're the best. I owe you." Taking Lynn's suggestion, I made a quick bathroom stop before heading to Quinn's office. I was going to tape the damn note to her desk to make sure it didn't get lost.

I was ten feet away from her office door when Justin, one of our newer groundskeepers, walked out and shut the door behind him.

Why was he in there? And where has he been? "Justin, is everything okay?"

He glanced over his shoulder, paled, and started walking away from me rather quickly.

I matched his pace. "Justin! Seriously, what's going on? Why were you in Quinn's office?"

He bolted for the exit door.

Oh hell no. Only guilty men run like that. I took off after him, quickly closing the distance, even while wearing heels and a pencil skirt. Growing up, I played football in skirts all the time with my brothers and cousins, and I had bested them more than once.

I chased Justin out of the side of the building into a small courtyard at full speed and football tackled him, a smile flitting across my face as he let out a satisfying thud and a wheeze when we both hit the ground. *Weren't expecting that, were you, asshole?*

When he started screaming obscenities and fighting me, nearly throwing me off his back, I reached back, took off my shoe, and hit him over the head. "Knock it off! You're the one who ran like a guilty man with his ass on fire. You brought this on yourself."

Just about the time he was about to buck me off him, Phil came sprinting out of the building. "Chels, are you okay?"

I grunted as Justin tried to throw me off his back again, and I struggled to keep his arms pinned behind him. "Just freaking peachy. I love nothing more than a casual sprint out of the building in the middle of winter, followed by a wrestling match with a wild boar. How about you do your damn job and help me out?"

"Yes, ma'am." There was a wicked smile forming on his lips, and I would be lying if it didn't make my stomach flutter.

Focus. This guy was messing with Quinn's office.

I shifted over and released my hold on the tackled idiot after Phil handcuffed him. Justin gave one final attempt to get away before getting efficiently knocked out with a swift punch from the muscular man who'd come running to my aid. It was both terrifying and impressive how well Phil did that, and with what looked like so little effort.

"I got here as fast as I could." He looked down at the guy, taking a moment to catch his breath. "Wait. What the hell? Why did you tackle Justin? Not that I'm upset we finally know where he is."

I looked at the man standing in front of me like he was insane. "You just knocked out and handcuffed a guy without questioning it?"

Phil shrugged. "I took the wild assumption you hadn't gone tearing out of the building after someone and beat them with your shoe because they were your best friend. I felt it was safe jumping to the assumption he was a bad guy."

Taking a deep breath, I wrapped my arms around myself in an attempt to stay warm and settle my nerves. "I went to put a note from a prospective client on Quinn's desk and found this *moron* sneaking out of it." I took another look at the unconscious idiot in the snow.

Phil nudged the guy with the toe of his boot, glaring at him. "What was he doing in her office?"

"No clue. When I called out to him, he took off like a bat out of hell, and instinct told me to follow."

"I'm glad you did."

Me, too.

"You two okay?"

I turned toward the male voice and saw Peter jogging toward us from the same door we both had run out of and nodded. "Yeah, we're fine. This guy," I gestured toward the man in the snow, "has seen better days, and won't see another if I have anything to say about it."

"Oh?" Peter tipped his head to the side as he took another look. "Oh shit. It's Justin!"

I nodded. "Anyone who messes with Quinn is immediately on my shit list, an employee of the lodge or not. Based on how he was acting, though, I have a gut feeling he was up to good."

"I won't bet against you there." Phil squatted down, tossed the guy over his shoulder, and stood up without so much of a grunt of effort.

How did he do that? He must lift weights. I wonder if he could pick me up like that. I shook my head. Now was *not* the time to be fantasizing.

"I'm going to find a place to secure him. You should get inside, Chels." He gave me a long look, long enough to make me want to run over to him and hug and kiss him again. The fact he had an unconscious Justin draped over his shoulder stopped me.

A soft cough pulled me from my thoughts and watching Phil walk away, was pulled back to the cruel reality that I had just tackled Justin after catching him leaving Quinn's office acting sketchy. *Her office!* "Shit. We need to get inside."

Peter slowly nodded as he watched me, a concerned expression on his face.

I ignored the unspoken question and rushed back toward the building. "Cold temperature aside, we need to check Quinn's office. He was coming out of there before I had to chase after him and catch him."

Chapter Seven

Chelsea

Peter and I ran into a frantic-looking Connor as we closed in on Quinn's office. "Chelsea, have you heard from or seen Quinn?"

I shook my head. "No. Isn't she in the ballroom, wrapping up her event?"

Without answering, he pushed Quinn's office door open and stopped a half-step into the room before letting out a frustrated groan. "No."

"What is it?"

"She's not in here. She told me she'd wait for me to come back."

How long have I been outside? "Was there anything in her office or on her desk? I saw Justin sneaking out of here earlier."

Connor and Peter quickly inspected the room, finding a torn corner from a red envelope taped to her monitor.

"Does she usually tape things to her screen?"

I shook my head. "Never. She hates anything sticking to her computer."

Connor frowned as took out his phone and then bit off a

swear. "Ryan just asked us to check for a piece of a red envelope in Quinn's office. Fuck."

"That fucker! I swear if Justin helped Jeffery hurt one hair on her head or laid a single finger on her, they are both going to wish Quinn's rage was the only thing they had to worry about."

Peter glanced over at me with an intrigued look on his face. "Not Lukas?"

I let out a derisive snort. "Peter, what's more terrifying to deal with: two pissed-off men or two pissed-off women?"

His eyes went wide. "Women. Hands down."

"I rest my case."

Peter nodded at me as Connor took off out of Quinn's office. "I need to get back to the security office. Can you lock her office and then stay at the desk?"

I leveled an annoyed glare at him, as echoes of the phone call with the nasty woman bounced around in my head. *What is it with people telling me what to do today?* "You mean, can I do my job?"

He opened and shut his mouth, before letting out a quick breath. "I'm sorry. That's not how I meant for it to come out. We need you at the desk for several reasons. One being so we know where you are in case we have to..."

"I know how to manage the lobby, Peter. How about you focus on *your* job? If it makes you both feel better, I promise not to leave my post unless I check in with one of you, okay?"

Peter nodded. "Again, I'm sorry and thank you." He walked me back to the lobby, and as calm as collected as he appeared to be, I didn't miss how his eyes were on a swivel.

Lynn shot me a confused look as I stepped behind the front desk. "What's going on? I was beginning to wonder where you'd gone off to, especially with Quinn and Connor going back and forth through here. You'd think there was some idiot trying to..."

She trailed off as her attention focused on me. "Oh, God, what happened now?"

Peter took a step closer to the desk. "You saw Quinn come through here?"

Lynn nodded. "Yeah, toward her office with Connor, and then back through here and out the back door without him a couple of minutes later. Lukas's sister came out of the elevator not too long after and headed out in the same direction Quinn went."

"Shit. Lianne headed out, too? How long ago was this?"

"Um... Maybe five minutes or so? I wasn't paying super close attention to the time."

"Noted." Peter immediately rushed off, probably toward the security office.

Lynn took a long look at me. "What in the hell happened to you?"

I glanced down at the front of my outfit, only then noticing the mud and wet spots all over me. *Well, shit.* "Um. Short version? I tackled Justin after catching him sneaking out of Quinn's office and chasing him down when he ran away like his pants were on fire."

Lynn's eyes went wide. "Wait. Justin? Like the guy who works in my department, Justin? The guy who's been MIA for like a week? What in the hell is going on here?"

"I have no idea, but it's way above my pay grade."

She snickered and shook her head. "Fair enough. I'm going to Edith. She's the top of the pay grade and might know something. I'll be back." Lynn took a few steps and then turned back to face me. "Do you have anything dry you can change into?"

I leaned down, reached into my cubby under the desk, and pulled out a spare cardigan I kept on hand for the days the foyer was cold. "I'll cover up with this, but thanks for looking out."

Once again, the lobby was empty, and I let out a slow breath. I knew Lukas and his guys were on top of whatever was happening, and there was little I could do to help. It didn't make me feel any better. Honestly, I felt like a sitting duck. I had no idea where the danger was or how to defend myself from it.

This sucks.

After answering several phone calls and taking down three reservations, a slightly older couple rushed into the building with two men close behind them.

"Are you Chelsea?"

Slightly stunned, I nodded at the gray-haired man now standing in front of my desk. I didn't know him, but there was something familiar about his eyes. "Yes? Can... Can I help you?"

He took a deep breath and let it out slowly. "Yes. I'm George Agosti. Lukas's dad. Ryan said you could point me in his direction."

Lukas's dad? The second he said it, the family resemblance immediately registered. "I... Um... Yes... Sorry. Right this way." I started to walk out from behind the desk when a very tense-looking Peter arrived in the lobby.

"Thanks, Chelsea. I'll take them from here. Mr. Agosti, Mrs. Agosti, right this way." He led them out of the lobby and in the direction of the security office.

Before I could even start to process that I'd just met Lukas's parents, the phone rang. It was an in-house call. "Front desk, this is Chelsea."

"Hi, this is Susan in room 323. Somehow our room was only stocked with washcloths and hand towels. Could we have some full-sized bath towels sent up?" There was a muffled giggle. "Apparently my husband didn't check before getting into the shower."

I did my best to suppress my own snicker, but I quickly

sobered. *How did that happen?* "Ma'am, I deeply apologize for that oversight. I'll call housekeeping immediately and have them brought up right away. I'd like to make it up to you by sending up some fresh-baked cookies."

There was another muffled giggle. "No need to apologize. I haven't laughed this hard in years. Though, I won't say no to the cookies I've heard so much about. Also, please don't feel the need to rush the towels. He'll figure it out."

I let out a relieved breath. "I'll still make sure to get those up as soon as I can." I made the mental note to send up milk and a carafe of hot chocolate as well.

"Thank you, Chelsea."

I ended the call and immediately called housekeeping and then the kitchen. Completing those very normal tasks helped settle my nerves, even if it bothered me that a guest room hadn't been properly stocked. The distraction was more than welcome as it kept me from completely freaking about whatever was going on with Quinn, Lukas, and Jeffery.

Taking advantage of the quiet and lack of guests around the lobby, I brought out the small vacuum and did a quick sweep of the area. It didn't really need it, but the noise and repetitive motion were calming. By the time I put everything away, I could almost pretend it was a normal day. Almost.

Phil

After I took Justin to the groundskeeping office, filled in Miles on the short version of the story, and helped him make sure Justin was adequately tied up, I headed back out, wanting to meet up with Peter. "I promise someone will be here as soon as we know more."

Miles nodded. "I've got this covered. Thanks, Phil."

I was making my way toward the security office, but sped up when I heard angry voices coming from behind the closed door. When I walked in, Liam was shouting at Borce, demanding answers. I couldn't help but notice his hair was still wet. *Figures he shows up once everyone has already headed out to help.* "What in the hell is going on *now*?"

The two turned toward me. Borce looked furious, and Liam looked like a petulant child who had been denied a Christmas present.

Borce stood up and took a step toward me. "This *gentleman*, if you can call him that, stormed in here, demanding I update him on everything going on, all while refusing to answer *any* of my questions."

"He's refusing to tell *me* what's happening."

I looked over at Liam and maintained the most neutral expression I could. *Whiny much?* "Where's Mr. Agosti?" A text had come in that he and Mrs. Agosti had arrived, but with all the chaos unfolding, I wanted to know exactly where everyone was.

Liam half rolled his eyes. "He's here, said he was heading toward the cabin with his guys, and told me to see what I could find out in here. I'm trying to, but *this man* refuses to cooperate."

I took a deep breath, trying to maintain my composure. "Since you've forgotten basic human decency, allow me to show you. This man is Borce. He happens to be the Director of Security here at Cardinal Hideaway. This is *his* domain, not ours. We are only allowed the *privilege* of working within *his* territory so long as we *cooperate* with him and the owners of the property. I'd appreciate if you'd stop trying to fuck up the good thing we have going on here." I returned my attention to Borce. "Allow me to introduce one of the men I have the displeasure of answering to. This is Liam Agosti, Lukas's older brother. Liam's wife recently had a baby, and the sleep deprivation has *clearly* robbed him of common sense and manners."

I was being rude, but I was beyond caring at the moment.

Borce shot me a look that told me of his current low opinion of Liam. "Thank you for answering the first and most basic question he refused to, thus confirming his identity. With all the unknown people and moles we've been dealing with, I was erring on the side of caution before handing over any information."

I nodded. "I greatly appreciate that. We all do. Speaking of information, any updates?"

"Yes." Borce returned to his chair and started typing on his keyboard. "I saw that brilliant tackle Chelsea made. Nice assist there, by the way."

When this is all over, I want to see that footage. "Thanks. We made a great team. Justin is tied up in the groundskeeping garage. Miles is watching him."

"Good to know." He clicked his mouse a couple of times and pulled up two different camera feeds. "When it comes to the whereabouts of Lukas, Quinn, and then Lianne, this is where we lose their trail. It's the west end of the property. If I had to guess I—"

"You aren't here to guess."

I looked over at Liam, who had just cut off Borce. "Not helpful, Liam. If you can't keep your mouth shut, go help your brother."

He glared at me. "Well... I don't know where he is."

No shit, Sherlock. "And Borce was *trying* to tell you before you jumped down his throat like an asshole. Can you cut the fucking power trip long enough so he can finish speaking, so I can figure out if there's anything I can do to make sure my boss stays alive? You can take up your complaints about my attitude with him once he's back." I took a deep breath and looked at the computer monitor again. "Isn't there an abandoned mine west of here?"

Borce nodded, trying to hide his amusement at my outburst.

"That's what I was going to say. I have a feeling that whatever is happening, *that's* where it's going down."

I took my phone out and texted the team. They may have put it together already, but knowledge, even conformation of it, was power.

Phil: < Head west. B and I agree about the old mine. >

Ryan: < Confirmed and on it. >

Where is Ryan right now?

"There are incoming visitors heading toward Quinn's cabin." Borce pulled up the feed, and I saw two men closing in on it as Connor waited and observed from the side of the building.

Shit. "I'm going in to back up Connor." I turned and glared at Liam. "I hope you enjoyed your shower. Wouldn't want you to have to get your hands dirty to help out your own brother."

Before he could respond, I was out of the security office and heading toward Connor's location. There were probably going to be consequences for my smart mouth, but they'd be worth it, especially if we all pulled through this alive.

Chapter Eight

Chelsea

I glanced at the clock, and realized check-in was soon and that I needed to make sure the reservations were ready to go, especially the packets for the cabin reservations.

I'd made my way half-way through the pile when low, angry voices came from the direction of the ballroom. My knees almost gave out a little when I saw a bloody, pissed off Lukas storm through the lobby with Quinn in his arms and Mrs. Agosti at their side.

What in the—Quinn! Lukas! What happened?

My head swam in panic at the sight of all the blood, cuts, and bruises burned into my mind, and the next thing I knew, there was an arm around my waist, keeping me from dropping to the ground.

"She's okay. They both are. It's going to be okay."

I jumped, nearly giving into the fight response at someone suddenly grabbing me, but relief washed over me at the familiar male voice, and I leaned against him. "You scared the shit out of me." *I'm glad you're here, though.*

An apologetic expression was all over Phil's face when I glanced up.

"Sorry, Chels. I would have asked before grabbing you, but I was more concerned with you hitting your head and getting hurt when your knees gave out like that."

"I appreciate it." I took a deep breath and let it out slowly, trying to calm myself as I stood on my own again. "Is Quinn really okay? You're not just saying that to make me feel better, are you?"

Phil kept an arm wrapped around my lower back, moving his thumb in small circles to comfort me. "I promise she's going to be okay, and from what little I've heard about what happened, she was a complete badass."

I let out a dry laugh and smoothed out the front of my skirt. "Well of course, she is. My Quinn is the epitome of badass. Only someone truly stupid would cross her."

"I've learned the same thing about you." He studied my face. "Are you sure *you're* okay? She's not the only one who's had a crazy day."

For the first time in my short time of knowing him, Phil actually looked freaked out. *Damn. How bad is it that even he's rattled?* "Yes, and no. I'm physically fine, but I can't say today has been a walk in the park."

He nodded in agreement. "You don't sprint through buildings and tackle idiots every day?"

A chuckle bubbled out of me, and some of the day's stress lightened. "No, I can't say I do."

Phil tipped his head to the side, a proud expression now on his face. "You're taking all of this so much better than almost anyone I've ever seen in a situation like this."

The tiniest amount of pride flickered in my chest. "This isn't the first time I've seen a jealous ex pull some crazy bullshit. This isn't even the first time I've run after someone and tackled them, or while wearing heels. However, this *is* the first time I've seen someone go *this* far to get someone else's attention, but some people are crazier than others. Jeffery happens to be more than a few fries short of a kid's meal, if you know what I mean."

"I won't disagree with you there." Phil chuckled and slid his hand up my back to pull me closer. "And you're really sure you're okay?"

I took a deep breath. "Before I can tell you that, answer this for me. Is this done now? At least for today?"

"I don't have all the details, but from what I know, it's over." He glanced around and leaned in, his lips nearly touching my ear. "Word is there's basically no one left to cause trouble anymore... if you catch my drift."

I gasped involuntarily. "Are they... dead?"

Phil shrugged. "I don't know the final numbers or details, but I will soon enough."

My attention shifted over to the closed elevator doors. "And you're *really* sure Quinn is going to be okay?" I finally had a kick-ass friendship with another woman actually worth calling a friend. The last thing I wanted was for her to be seriously hurt.

As if on cue, there was a ding from the elevators and a determined-looking Mrs. Agosti walked out, glancing around the lobby. When her attention locked on Phil, she beelined in his direction.

"Phil, do we have an ETA on the medical backup?"

He stood up straight, dropped his arm from my back to my waist, and nodded. "Yes, ma'am. Doc is en route from the airport, and Borce pulled a few strings to get a couple of off-duty paramedics here. They should arrive any minute."

The older woman nodded. "Good. Where's Liam?"

Phil opened and shut his mouth twice before responding. "I just came from the security room where he was being rude to Borce, the chief of security here at the lodge. Before then I believe he, Susan, and the baby were in their suite."

Her eyebrows went up. "He was in his room while all of this was going on?"

"Yes, ma'am. From what I heard."

That cannot be a coincidence. "Wait, did you say Susan?"

Phil looked at me curiously and nodded. "Do you know her?"

"She called down a little bit ago asking for more towels."

A frustrated growl came out of Phil. "And Liam's hair was still wet when I ran into him."

Mrs. Agosti inhaled sharply and let it out slowly as she shook her head. "May God have mercy on him."

I was confused and looked between the two of them. "Did something happen to him, too?" *Is that the reason she needed towels? Had he gotten hurt and needed to clean up? Why would she have laughed about it?*

The woman gave me a sympathetic smile. "Not yet, my dear. He's made some interesting choices today that will undoubtedly earn him the ire of at least his brother. Whatever rage-induced storm he has coming his way because of it, he will have earned fair and square. Honestly, I'll be surprised if my husband doesn't get an earful and will have to break up a fight between those two before all the dust settles." She took a deep breath and stood a bit taller as if trying to shake off the insanity of the day. "Chelsea, do you know if Edith's chef is in the kitchen?"

"Allen? Yeah. He's been here for a couple of hours. Why?"

"Excellent. I need something, and I think he can help me. "

Phil stepped out from behind the counter. "Would you like me to walk there with you?"

She patted him on the arm. "Thank you for asking, my dear, but that's not necessary. The immediate danger has been taken care of, and my dear husband and children aren't the only ones with tricks up their sleeves." Without another word, she turned on her heel and headed toward the kitchen.

The woman was a force to be reckoned with. *I want to be like her when I grow up.* I glanced over at Phil, and my thoughts went to Lukas. "Why do I get the impression world war three is going to break out between Liam and Lukas?"

"Because it just might."

"Gotcha." For once, I wasn't sure if I wanted to be anywhere near them when it happened.

He walked over to my side again. "You never answered my question before. Are you okay?"

I nodded and gave him a small smile. "If Mrs. Agosti is confident enough to leave Lukas and Quinn for whatever the kitchen holds, I am peachy keen holding down the fort at my desk."

"I knew I liked you... a lot." Phil rubbed my shoulder, kissed the side of my head, turned, and headed back toward the security office.

Wait. A lot?

Phil

I had been planning to check in with Borce, but seeing Liam heading toward the groundskeeping office piqued my interest. My phone buzzed in my pocket.

Peter: < Mr. A and I are chatting with Miles and keeping an eye on J. >

Phil: < I'm en route. Liam is just ahead of me. >

Peter: < Noted. >

I caught up with Liam just as he walked through the office and into the garage attached to it.

He glanced at the man tied up and strapped to a metal folding chair. "Who's this?"

"Justin White."

The fury and disdain in Miles's voice was acidic and caught

me off guard. I'd never heard him say a mean, or mean *sounding*, word the entire time I'd been here.

Liam shot a confused look at him. "And *why* is he tied up and being held here?"

Mr. Agosti cleared his throat, shooting a pointed look at his oldest son. "Not only is he part of the team that knocked out and abducted your brother, he's also the one who planted something in Quinn's office that sent her racing out of the building to rescue him. Apparently something was communicated with Lianne, who headed out shortly thereafter. Since I've arrived, we've confirmed not only is he connected to Jeffery, he was also one of the people involved in the nasty job of burying Quinn in that icy coffin Lukas saved her from."

It took everything in me not to immediately beat the shit out of Justin. "Does Lukas know we have him?"

"Not yet, but he will when I get the chance to talk to him."

I nodded at Mr. Agosti. "Excellent."

"Why are we waiting?"

We all looked at Liam, confused.

Peter cleared his throat. "Correct me if I'm wrong, but I'm assuming Mr. Agosti is waiting to act until he's had a chance to debrief Lukas, Quinn, Lianne, Ryan, and Connor."

Liam showed the first signs of concern. "Ryan *and* Connor went out there, too? Without all the information? That's reckless."

The most senior Agosti nodded. "They did. Once we figured out some of what was going on, Borce pulled up camera footage. Not only was Lukas abducted, Quinn was also abducted, again. Lianne, and then Ryan, were quick to arrive at her cabin before disappearing in the same corner of the camera's view." He glanced over at this son. "And where were *you* during all of this?"

"Fucking around in the shower."

We all turned to see Chelsea standing in the doorway with her hands on her hips, glaring in Liam's direction.

As much as I was shocked by her statement, I tensed up at her sudden appearance. *Now what happened? Why did she leave the front desk? Who's there now?* "Is everything okay?"

Her expression softened slightly as she glanced my way, but the rage was still there. "Your bosses, coworkers, and family are certainly keeping my lobby hopping today. Connor walked in, and just as I was starting to pepper him with questions, two of Borce's paramedic friends strolled in and cut me off. Connor took one of them to the ballroom to look over Frank and Ryan, and had the other wait with me. Not even a minute later, a man named Doc walked up to the desk the same time Lianne rushed out of the elevator and into the lobby. She told me to tell you about the paramedics and that she was taking one up to check over Quinn and having Doc check over Lukas." Chelsea took a deep breath and glanced up at the ceiling as she let it out slowly. "I think that was everything I was supposed to tell you." Her attention shifted down to Justin and then over to me. "Can I finish what I started with this piece of shit?"

Mr. Agosti let out a small chuckle as he stepped forward. "My apologies, Chelsea. I feel like I was rude earlier when my wife and I arrived and I brushed you off without a proper introduction. I'm George Agosti."

She shook his offered hand, giving him a curious but friendly look. "It's a pleasure to meet you, sir. There's no reason to apologize. You did introduce yourself. Honestly, even if it hadn't been this much of a chaotic day, you were still more polite than a good quarter of the guests I've checked in."

"Still, my mother raised me with manners, and I wanted to make sure I used them." He gave her a rare smile. "I hear you're the one to thank for the capture of this individual."

"I am, and you're welcome."

He chuckled, stunning me slightly. "Thank you, and while I appreciate all your assistance and... enthusiasm, I need him alive a little longer."

Chelsea grinned and was about to respond when Liam cut her off.

"This is *Agosti* business, miss. You need to head back to the front desk and make sure the phone gets answered."

Chelsea is going to kill Liam for saying that. I inhaled sharply and prepared to stop whatever assault I was sure would be coming from her.

She put her hands on her hips again and glared at him. "I don't give a *shit* about who's business *you* think this is. I don't even know or *care* who you are. I'm not going anywhere. I have just as much of a right to be in the groundskeeping office and garage as you do, if not more. Besides, *you're* not my boss. *You* don't have the privilege of telling me what to do. You want me out of here? Get my boss to tell me. Oh, wait. He's getting checked out by paramedics right now."

I thought Chelsea had been impressive before, but now I felt like I was in the presence of true power and greatness. I wanted to kiss and worship every inch of the goddess before me. There was something so very attractive about a woman who could hold her own, but her chewing out Liam was just the whipped topping gracing the gloriously delicious dish that was Chelsea, a dish I wanted to savor. *Now is not the time for that.*

Liam let out an irritated, almost bored-sounding sigh and looked in my direction. "Phil, get her out of here. She needs to be where she belongs. Not in here, getting in the way of what happens next."

"I really think you should head back to the lobby, Chelsea."

Her attention rested on me briefly, and I begged her with my eyes to comply. Those fiery blue eyes locked on Liam again as she walked up and stood toe-to-toe with him and poked him in the chest. "You. Aren't. My. Boss."

"Sweetie, this may be difficult for you to understand, but—"

The stunning right hook Chelsea threw at Liam cut off his demeaning sentence and had him taking a few steps backward.

"Fuck you and your misogynistic bullshit."

Blood was already dripping from his split lip as she was pulling back for another hit. *Oh shit.* I rushed forward, crouched down, caught her on my shoulder, and stood up, stopping her from punching him again, not that he didn't deserve it.

Chelsea pounded on my shoulders and back with her fists repeatedly as I walked toward the door. "Put me down! I wasn't done."

I tightened my grip on the back of her thighs and calves, making sure she didn't throw herself off me. "I will in a sec." *Once I have you in another room far away from Liam. Not that he doesn't deserve more of that.*

Peter opened the door to the hall for me, nodded, and closed it again once we were through it and in the hallway. As much as I wanted to be in there and have Lukas's back, especially since he wasn't able to be in there to stop his brother from trying to take over, I knew keeping Chelsea and Liam away from each other was probably the most helpful thing I could do right now. Mr. Agosti already had his hands full and didn't need more drama piled on.

She was still ranting when I opened the door and walked into my hotel room, setting her down on the bed.

"That egotistical, pompous, self-righteous pain in the ass. And *you!* You were no help! Dragging me out of there like some child. I could have taken him."

I looked down at her, slowly rubbing the sides of her shoulders with my hands. "I have no doubt you would have given Liam quite a run for his money."

Chelsea's jaw dropped open, and her blue eyes went wide. "Holy Shit. I punched Lukas's brother in the face."

I nodded, amused by her reaction.

She let out a deep breath. "I can't believe I went off on him like that. I mean, I *can* believe it, but... No. I'm not going to feel bad or apologize for putting him in his place and giving him a little reality check. I don't care what family he comes from. That man was completely out of line."

Chelsea was quickly becoming my favorite person ever.

Suddenly, she stood up again. "This changes things. I need to go back and finish yelling at Liam. He is not the boss of this place. I don't care how many people he charms, yells at, or tries to intimidate."

I shook my head and moved to block the door so she couldn't get out. "They are taking care of business."

Chelsea glared at me. "Yeah, *Frank* and *Edith's* business. I've been here a hell of a lot longer than he has. Why does Liam think he can walk in here and act like he owns the freaking place? At least Lukas had the decency to ask first and *not* assume he was in charge." She ineffectually shoved at me and got more frustrated, frantic, and upset. "Why won't you move? I need to get out of here." Chelsea let out a pained whine. "Fine. Forget Liam. I need to make sure Quinn is okay. I need to make sure Frank is okay. I need to make sure my people are okay."

The rising panic in her voice both surprised me and didn't. I shook my head. "I need to keep you here, Chelsea."

She shoved me again. "Says who?"

I let out a deep sigh and wrapped my arms around her, holding her tight until she stopped fighting. "Come on, Chels. You know I can't let you back in that room, and if you stop and think about it, you know *why* you can't go back in that room. I also can't let you go racing to wherever they stashed Lukas and Quinn and Frank. The medical professionals need space and privacy to do their jobs."

She sighed and leaned into me. "I know. I still hate him."

"I know. I'm not fond of him, either."

"I'm talking about Liam... and Jeffery... and Justin... and anyone else mixed up in this crap."

"Oh, I know. And you're not the only one worried about Lukas, Quinn, and Frank." I was also worried about Lianne, Ryan, and Connor. We'd been damn lucky no one had been too seriously hurt. Today was too close of a call.

Chelsea leaned into me a little more. "True. I'm still pissed that he thinks he can boss me around."

I rested the side of my cheek on the top of her head. "We all went through a lot today. I agree Liam could have, and probably should have, handled it differently."

"He's a stupid asshole." The words were grumbled into my chest.

Thank you for saying what I can't... well, shouldn't. "I won't argue with you there. How are you feeling now?"

She let out a long breath and tipped her head up to look at me. "Better than before, but still not great. I can't get the image of a bloody Quinn and Lukas walking through the lobby out of my head."

Same. "You need another minute?"

"Yeah."

The muscles in her back were tensing up again, and her grip on my shirt tightened. "Coming off that adrenaline rush?" Chelsea nodded, and my chest tightened in sympathy. "I've got you. You can stay here as long as you need to."

"But... The front desk—"

"Is being covered." I cut her off and kissed the top of her head. "You can take all the time you need. I'll take any heat."

"Thank you." Her voice was quiet as she stood there, still leaning into me.

This was more the reaction I'd been expecting from her. "You want to sit down or stay here?"

Chelsea wrapped her arms around my waist, squeezing a little. "Here is good."

A guy could get used to holding her like this.

Chapter Nine

Phil

Eventually Chelsea was to a point where she could leave the room and finish her day. After I walked her to the front desk, I gave her one last quick side hug. "Text me if you need anything, okay?"

She nodded. "Will do. And thank you for earlier."

I squeezed her hand "I've got your back, Chelsea. If you start feeling like that again, I'm more than happy to help you through it."

"Thanks." A tiny smile appeared on her face as she nodded.

Movement in my periphery caught my attention, and I grinned and headed over when I saw Edith walking toward the elevator with a basket in her arms. "Treats for Lukas and Quinn?"

The older woman gave me a tight smile and a small nod. "Now that I know my Frank is okay, I need to check on my girl."

"Would you like me to escort you there?"

Edith stared at me for a moment before shaking her head. "You make sure my lobby stays safe. I know there are plenty of eyes on the third floor at the moment. Besides," she glanced over my shoulder, "I think Chelsea might feel better knowing you're nearby. I heard about who she found and the glorious tackle."

"You have some very loyal employees, Ms. Edith."

A scowl appeared on her face. "I thought we did. Justin has made quite the fool out of us."

The elevator dinged and the doors slid open. "Don't let one bad kid question your judgment."

Edith walked into the elevator car and turned, tipping her head to the side. "Are you saying that to convince you or me?"

Her words pulled a chuckle from me. "Both."

"Glad to see you being honest about that." With a smirk on her lips, the doors slid shut again and the hydraulic jack kicked on, sending her up to the third floor.

Several laps around the main entrance, foyer, Reading Room, and adjacent hallways later, Edith returned to the lobby and was chatting with Chelsea. I watched the two women interact and the weight lifted from my shoulders when they both looked far more relaxed.

When it was time for Chelsea to go home, I walked her out to her car. "Text or call me when you get home and then when you're in your house. Please."

An amused grin appeared on her face. "I'm beginning to think you like hearing from me."

"I do." I couldn't keep the grin off my face.

"Good, and I will."

Unable to stop myself, I pulled her into a hug. "You were magnificent today."

Chelsea leaned into me and hugged me back. "Thanks."

We stood there for a moment before my phone buzzed, startling us both and pulling us from the moment. She chuckled and shook her head. "Here's hoping we all have an uneventful night."

"Agreed."

I waited until Chelsea was in her car and driving away before pulling my phone out.

Ryan: < Red and L are heading back to the cabin. Full escort request. C is already in place. >

Phil: < I'm out front and will skirt around the west side of the main building and meet up. >

Ryan: < Thanks. >

By the time I made it to the back of the building, Lukas, Quinn, and Ryan had just walked out of the back door. I fell in step behind and just to the right of Quinn while Ryan took a similar position with Lukas and we slowly and silently made our way to her cabin.

Between the slow pace and the death grip Quinn had on Lukas, I could tell she was in pain and barely handling the events of the day, but her strength and fierce determination was awe-inspiring. It reminded me a lot of Chelsea's strength.

It was truly an honor to be in the presence of so many strong women.

When we finally made it to the cabin, I was fully expecting Quinn and Lukas to walk in. About twenty feet from the front steps of the porch, Quinn halted. "Ryan, Phil, take a walk and check around the house."

"Connor just checked—"

"Do it again." Quinn's sharp words cut off Lukas's response.

Ryan and I glanced at Lukas, and after a subtle nod from him, the two of us methodically made our way around the small cabin, taking in the hundreds of footprints surrounding the building. There wasn't anything new there, as we all knew, but I was happy to make Quinn feel safer in her own home.

When we returned to the front of the building, Ryan stepped closer to Quinn. "Nothing to report. The perimeter of the cabin and property are clear and secure."

Quinn didn't move. "Thank you. Now, inside."

I caught Lukas's nod, and Ryan and I headed past Connor.

Ryan clapped his hand on his shoulder as we passed him. "Good work today." Connor's response was a curt nod.

Once the cabin had been cleared on the inside, and Lukas and Quinn had settled in, Ryan and I headed back to the lodge after Connor *insisted* he needed to stay there for a while longer.

We were barely out of earshot when Ryan glanced my way. "I'm going to crash for a few hours and then relieve him around midnight."

"I can relieve you at six if you'd like."

He nodded. "Much appreciated."

Later that night, after I was back in my room, I couldn't keep a grin off my face as I reread the tiny text conversation between me and Chelsea

Chelsea: < Home safe and sound. :) >

Phil: < Good to hear. Let me know if you need anything. >

Chelsea: < I think I can manage a night without you having to come save the day. >

Phil: < I know you don't need saving. I said I'd be here if you needed something.

Phil: < Just like the mistletoe. >

Chelsea had impressed the hell out of me the way she tackled Justin earlier. I knew she was strong, but that was a whole new level I never expected from her. Thank God she had been in the right place at the right time. Her help in catching Justin made me appreciate her that much more. There were guys I'd worked with who wouldn't have tried that move. Beating the man over his head with her shoe had been a nice touch.

And then there was her heated, no-nonsense interactions with both Liam and Mr. Agosti. The momentary stunned look on Liam's face when she went off on him was something I would cherish forever.

Chelsea was an amazing woman, and one I wanted to get to know more. Sure, we'd bantered, chatted, and flirted back and forth for a few weeks now, and today was the most physical contact I'd ever had with her, but I craved more of it. Sitting on my bed and leaning my head against the headboard, I let out a deep sigh.

"You're thinking pretty hard over there. Everything okay?"

I looked over at Peter. "Oh, um, yeah. I'm good. Today was nuts."

He let out a low whistle. "You can say that again. I'm glad it ended with all of our guys mostly upright."

"Me, too." Lukas had looked pretty roughed up, but I knew he was way more concerned about Quinn's state.

"Chelsea's contributions were an unexpected, but very welcome, surprise."

I nodded in agreement. "That they were. I knew there was more to her than we'd seen, but I would have never guessed tackling Justin, getting into a shouting match with Liam, and then punching him would be on her list of abilities."

Peter chuckled. "I don't know if you caught it, but Mr. Agosti actually smirked when Chelsea went off on Liam. Hell, it was hard for *me* to keep a straight face."

A smile appeared on my face. "I missed that. I was too stunned by what she said to look around."

"Fair. I'm glad Lianne wasn't there to hear what her brother said. She would have *definitely* had something to say about that."

"Kind of like what Chelsea did?"

Peter nodded. "Speaking of, I heard it was a while before Chelsea came back to the front desk. What happened after you got her out of the office?"

"After her rage toward Liam and the general adrenaline rush wore off, she crashed pretty hard, mentally. Honestly, I'm shocked it took her that long. I kept her in here until she was as good as she could be before walking her back."

"You kept her here and made her feel better?" He arched an eyebrow, the knowing twinkle in his eye giving away his assumptions.

I flipped him off. "It wasn't like that. This was the first place I could think of that wasn't a public place or in the way of medical staff. I had a feeling once the anger fizzled out, she was going to need a quiet, private place to vent her frustrations and have an adrenaline crash or something."

"No, it was a great plan. You two have been getting closer the past few weeks, and I'm glad you were able to help her out. I'm not sure it would have been as well-received if any of the rest of us would have tried to help her."

Eventually Peter gave up trying to watch the TV show he had on and laid down, probably to try to get some sleep. He was supposed to work later, but if my gut feeling was correct, Mr. Agosti was going to send him back to bed once his team had been filled in and given the grand tour of the security end of the property. I went back to the book I had been reading for the past week, and I was only two pages in when my thoughts returned to the blond bombshell I wanted to wrap my arms around again.

I loved how it felt to hold her. There was a comfort in being the person to be there when her world was crumbling around her.

It was one thing to be a bodyguard and have it be my job to protect someone, but it was entirely different to want to keep someone safe simply because they were important to you. It was a feeling I hadn't known I'd been missing, but now that I knew what it felt like, I needed more. I needed *her*.

Chapter Ten

Chelsea

As promised, I texted Phil when I got home.

Chelsea: < Home safe and sound. :) >

Phil: < if you need anything, let me know. >

What I need is a way to forget just enough of today to be able to sleep. I slowly let out a tense breath and focused on what I needed to do next. Eat.

Chelsea: < I think I can manage a night without you having to come save the day. >

Phil: < Regardless, I'm here. >

Phil: < So is the mistletoe. >

With a chuckle and an eye roll, I headed into my kitchen for my favorite comfort food combo: tater tots, chicken nuggets, and a vodka drink. My phone buzzed again, and a wide grin appeared on my face when I saw my best friend's name.

June: < I've been hearing all kinds of wild and crazy stories about your lodge tonight. What in the hell happened over there? >

I stared at the screen, knowing I didn't have the mental bandwidth to get into the entire story with her. After thinking for a moment, I texted her back.

Chelsea: < Today was nuts, but I'm wiped and about to eat tots and nuggies in a bubble bath while enjoying another Moscow Mule. >

June: < Damn. The comfort trifecta? That must have been a rough day. Can you fill me in later… when you're allowed? >

Chelsea: < 100%. I promise the lodge is quite safe and sound. I'm fine. It's business as usual for anyone asking. >

June: < I got ya, bestie! Enjoy your night. >

By the time my food was done cooking, I was on my second Moscow Mule and ready for a long soak in the tub. The hope was that between the hot bath and the liquor, I'd wash away or numb all the insanity, at least for the night.

I dug around in the bottom of my linen closet and pulled out the Epsom salt and the lavender bubble bath. I was using every trick I had in the book to make this the most relaxing evening. I even pulled out my tablet and started playing one of my favorite 'chill-out' playlists.

By the time I sank into the sea of bubbly tranquility, my food was gone, and I was feeling the effects of the alcohol. Even with the music playing, it was still pretty quiet, and my thoughts started to race, replaying scenes from the day.

Well, shit.

Without thinking about why, I grabbed my phone from the safety of the closed toilet lid and texted the only person I figured would get it.

Chelsea: < My brain won't stop. >

I didn't expect his immediate response or how happy I was to see it pop in.

Phil: < You and me both. >

**Chelsea: < Even though this is literally your job?
>**

**Phil: < I may be trained to protect and stop things
like that from happening, but it doesn't make it any
less stressful to deal with during or after all the dust
settles. >**

Phil: < It helps to distract yourself. >

Without thinking about it, I took a picture of my feet sticking
out of the bubbles and sent it.

**Chelsea: < I've made and ate some of my favorite
comfort food … made one of my favorite drinks…
have my favorite music playing… sitting in a bubble
bath… I swear none of it is helping. >**

A picture popped up. It was Phil's legs from the knees down
on one of the hotel beds, ankles crossed. He was barefoot and
wearing blue and green plaid pajama pants. There was the part of
an open book in the bottom of the image. *He reads?*

**Chelsea: < You look all cozy. Doing anything fun?
>**

**Phil: < I was trying to read, but it's not going well.
There's nothing I want to watch on TV right now,
either. I totally get the restless thing tonight. >**

Phil: < Talking to you is nice, though. :) >

The biggest grin appeared on my face as a tiny, excited squeal
came out.

Chelsea: < I like talking to you, too. >

I sank into the water a little more and prayed I didn't drop my
phone in the tub. That was the last thing I needed.

**Phil: < So how long do you soak before you're
done? I've never really tried the whole bubble bath**

thing, and I have no idea how it's supposed to work.
>

A giggle bubbled out as I thought about his question. *Are there actual rules?*

Chelsea: < Well, for me, I stay in until I get bored or until the water gets too chilly. Whichever happens first. >

Phil: < That makes sense. How's it going tonight? >

I let out a deep sigh as I looked around and.

Chelsea: < I'll probably get out soon. It's not as relaxing me as much as I'd like, and I'm just getting antsy. >

Phil: < Then what's the new plan? >

That was something I'd not considered. This was the first time the trifecta hadn't worked.

Chelsea: < I have no clue. >

Phil: < You want to call me when you're out of the tub and changed into something comfortable? >

A snicker popped out before I responded.

Chelsea: < Is this some weird way to get a dirty phone call? >

Phil: < Actually, no. I legit meant pajamas or whatever comfortable clothes you wanted to lounge in. >

Phil: < and if I wanted a dirty call, I wouldn't be waiting for you to get dressed. ;) >

Chelsea: < LOL Fair enough. Yeah, I'll call. Give me ten, maybe fifteen minutes? >

Phil: < Take all the time you need. >

I put the phone back in its safe place and let out a slightly annoyed breath. It wasn't because of Phil. It was more frustrating that I needed someone to help me process the day.

You help your friends out all the time. How is this any different? Does it matter that it's the man I'm kind of obsessed with?

Not wanting to deal with myself and my thoughts anymore, I rinsed off while the tub drained. Once I was in my favorite cozy pajamas and all curled up in bed, I dialed Phil's number.

"You called."

A chuckle came out as I settled in against my pillow. "Of course I did. Why do you sound so surprised?"

"I wasn't sure if I scared you off with the dirty call comment."

I shook my head. "This coming from the man who not only gave me the most glorious kiss today, but also held me later when I was losing my shit? I feel like I'd be the one scaring you away at this point."

"Nah, you'd have to do a lot more than that to scare me away. Regardless, how are you feeling now? Any better?"

I took a deep breath and let it out slowly. "I mean... Yeah, but no."

"I get that. You want to be distracted by an absolutely ridiculous story about Liam?"

More dirt on the idiot I punched earlier? "Oh my god, yes, please. Wait, won't you wake up Peter? He's still in your room, right?"

"Peter is working right now, so I won't be disturbing anyone. Anyway, the story about Liam. After his daughter was born, the sleep deprivation was real. Chloe had colic and refused to sleep unless someone was holding her, and he and Susan were at their wit's end. He was still technically on paternity leave, but came in for some meeting, and guess what he was wearing."

I sat up with a delighted gasp. "What?"

"One of Susan's shirts."

"No way! Are you sure? There isn't always a huge difference between men's and women's t-shirts."

Phil's loud chuckle brought an even bigger smile to my face. "It wasn't just a t-shirt. He was wearing one of her pregnancy shirts, glitter scripted words and all."

I fell over into my side, cry-laughing at the mental image. The second I caught my breath, he immediately launched into another story about some ridiculous prank Lukas tried to pull on Lianne that backfired in his face. This led to us sharing stories about all the ridiculous people we'd had to work or deal with.

I'm not sure how long we talked, but at some point I fell asleep. The only reason I knew was when I woke up a few hours later and found my phone with nine percent left on the battery and a text message.

Phil: < Sleep well :) >

After plugging in my phone, I did just that.

Phil

I was surprised when Chelsea had texted me. I was even more surprised when she called me back after her bubble bath. Hearing her calm down and laugh more as we talked put the biggest smile on my face, and the pride that coursed through me when she finally relaxed enough to fall asleep was like none other. It felt better than almost every other successful mission I'd completed.

After texting her good night, I rolled over and went to sleep, not at all upset that I was only going to get a handful of hours in before relieving Ryan. It was more than worth it. One short night of sleep wasn't going to hurt me. Besides, Edith had amazing coffee. I'd be fine.

The next morning, my alarm went off at 5:30am and Edith, like she had for weeks, had a carafe of fresh coffee waiting. After filling to-go cups for me and Ryan, I headed over to the cabin and arrived at about ten minutes to six.

"Here. Something to keep you upright."

Ryan took the cup from me with a grateful smile. "Thanks."

"Anything happen last night?"

He shook his head. "Nope. Everything was quiet for both me and Connor. And with that, I'm going to head into the security office, finish compiling my report about yesterday, and maybe talk with George. Thanks for the coffee."

I took a walk around the cabin, confirming that everything was fine, and then settled into one of the chairs on the porch and drank my coffee, content to enjoy the sunrise. I had only been out there about an hour and a half before Gage walked up. I gave him a curious look. "Hey. What's up?"

"George sent me out here to relieve whoever was camped out."

"I appreciate that, but I relieved Ryan a little over an hour ago."

Gage gave me a level stare. "Phil, it's not an option. Between you and me, the man is feeling a lot of guilt over everything that happened yesterday. He wants to do what he can to help out, even if it's after the fact. Also, you look like hell."

I laughed and ran my hand through my messy hair. "I didn't think it was that bad."

He clapped his hand on my shoulder. "Go, have a hot breakfast, drink something warm, and enjoy a few moments of peace before wedding chaos erupts."

My eyes went wide. *Holy shit! There's supposed to be a wedding tomorrow.* "Is it still on?"

Gage shrugged. "I haven't heard either way. I'm sure Lianne and Ben will let everyone know one way or the other ASAP. In the meantime, go."

"Yes, sir." I nodded and gave a little mock salute before

heading toward the lodge. While technically I didn't have to do anything the man told me, it was the unwritten rule that George Agosti had the final say in many things. If he wanted to give me the morning off, I wasn't going to fight it.

Walking back into the kitchen in hopes of something to eat, I was surprised to see someone other than Edith pulling a tray of cinnamon rolls out of the oven. "Mrs. Agosti?"

She turned and flashed me a smile. "Oh, good. Gage got you to leave. Have a seat, sweetie."

Too stunned to do anything else, I immediately complied. "Um... Where's Edith?"

Mrs. Agosti turned to continue making what looked like frosting for the cinnamon rolls she'd just pulled out of the oven. "She's in the ballroom setting up a few things for us to have breakfast in there. Lianne already texted Quinn about it, but Edith made an executive decision per my request. After the chaos that descended on the lodge yesterday, I wanted to separate our family and whatever drama the morning brought from the lodge guests." She took a deep breath and let it out slowly. "Oh, there's a fresh pot of coffee ready. Go on, pour yourself a mug."

"Yes, ma'am." As I refilled my cup, a thought hit me. "Do you know if Chelsea is here?"

"She is, actually. She strolled through here not that long ago and grabbed a muffin for herself. Edith told her she shouldn't have been here for another several hours, if it all, but Chelsea insisted she wanted to come in and take care of a few breakfast and wedding-related things for Quinn's ... Oh, how did she put it?" Mrs. Agosti glanced up at the ceiling for a moment. "That's right. Chelsea was doing this so that when Frank got Lukas to turn off Quinn's alarm and inform her she had the day off today, there would be fewer arguments as to why she couldn't be here."

My heart warmed when I heard about Chelsea coming in early. "So the wedding is still happening?"

Mrs. Agosti laughed as she frosted the tray of cinnamon rolls. "Oh, yes. Lianne was *insistent* that everything go on as planned. I believe she said something to the effect of, 'no idiot is going to stop me from having my wedding day,' or something. I didn't argue with her. My children don't waver once their minds are made up, for better or for worse."

"No ma'am, they don't. Well, I'm going to bring Chelsea a mug of coffee."

"She takes hers with three french vanilla creamers and two packets of sugar."

I glanced up at Edith, who gave me a knowing wink as she walked into the kitchen. "Thanks."

"Anytime, my dear. You should also take some cinnamon rolls with you."

"Yes, ma'am." She didn't have to tell me twice. Those things would end the ugliest of wars. *Would they make the Agosti siblings get along better? That might be too much pressure to put on a pastry.*

Feeling confident, knowing I made a mug of coffee Chelsea would actually like, I made my way to the front desk first to see if she was there. I was only slightly surprised to see Damien standing there. "Don't you typically stick to working the overnights?"

He smirked as he glanced up. "I do, but Chelsea asked a favor, and I'm not above working a little overtime here and there. If you're looking for her, she said she'd be in Quinn's office for a bit.

"Thanks." I made my way over to the other hallway and down to Quinn's open office door. A smile spread across my face when I saw Chelsea standing behind the desk, looking intently at the computer screen. "I come bearing caffeine and sugar."

She jumped a little, and then shot me a playful glare while reaching for the mug of coffee closest to her. "If you didn't have coffee, I'd have to hurt you. Wait, did you say sugar? Do I smell cinnamon rolls?"

"Yep." I grinned as I sat a plate with two of the pastries on the desk in between us. "Can I join you before everyone is awake and the full chaos of whatever today is going to hold kicks in?"

Chelsea's eyes twinkled as she smiled and took a sip from her mug. "I'd be insulted if you didn't."

Chelsea

We'd been setting up and decorating the ballroom for a couple hours when Lianne returned from taking a phone call. "Quinn, please go take a break. I know this is your room and your domain, and I'm not trying to tell you how to do your job, but please relax. Yesterday was a lot, and tomorrow is going to be just as energy consuming, though hopefully less chaotic. Ben and I are also taking a break before the rehearsal while the rest of the party and family arrive, and I'd feel so much better if you did, too. There's nothing else that needs to happen between now and then."

Quinn looked around the room, and I nodded when she met my gaze. Lianne wasn't wrong. The ballroom looked amazing.

"Fine, but only since you asked so nicely."

Lianne gave her a quick hug. "Thank you. Now, I'm probably not supposed to say anything, but I think Lukas has a surprise cooked up for you at your cabin."

Quinn's eyebrows shot up. "Oh? You're speaking to him again?"

The bride-to-be laughed. "Yep. He informed me he formally asked you to be his date. I also know he's up to something adorable to woo you some more, and I wholeheartedly approve of that. Go have some fun. I'll see you at 5:30pm." Lianne gave Quinn a gentle nudge toward the door, making her chuckle.

"That goes for you, too, Chelsea."

It was my turn to chuckle when Lianne gave me a playful glare. "Yes, ma'am."

Phil sauntered over to my side as I walked through the lobby to go have my prescribed fun. "Where are you off to?"

He just appears out of thin air sometimes, I swear. "Lianne told me and Quinn to take a break. So I was thinking of visiting June at the bar for a bit before I have to come back."

"That sounds like fun."

I paused, taking advantage of a moment of courage. "Would you like to join me?"

His face lit up, and he grabbed his phone. "Hold on a sec." After sending a few texts, he looked up. "Let's go. I'll drive."

While I was a little stunned when Phil immediately wanted to and could join me. I was by no means going to complain about it. *I need to chill out. It's just the two of us hanging out.*

Phil

Peter and I had been to the bar a few times since coming out to Colorado, but going with Chelsea, and especially knowing I was going to meet her best friend, made me more nervous than I wanted to admit. Then there was everything else lodge and work related. *Getting a drink is sounding better and better.*

"You okay?"

I glanced at her and nodded before returning my attention to the road. "I'm great. Why?"

"Really?" Her dry tone told me she wasn't buying it. "You want to try that again?"

Not wanting to make a big deal of it, I shrugged. "There's a lot of pieces in motion right now, and we are trying to keep things moving as smoothly as possible while also keeping everyone safe."

Chelsea nodded. "So you're stressing out, too. Good."

"Good?" That was not the response I'd been expecting.

"Yep. Good. Only someone heartless or emotionless would be unbothered by all this." She reached over and gave my arm a squeeze. "I'm glad you're normal."

"Thank you?" *That's a good thing, right?*

A delightful chuckle bubbled out of her. "It was supposed to be a compliment. I like that you're human and aren't completely unshakeable. Honestly, it's relieving to know you can get stressed out and rattled and that there's more than ice in your veins."

I pulled into the parking lot, choosing to park in one of the spots farther down from the door. After turning off the car, I turned to face Chelsea. "I have to look calm, cool, and collected at work. How reassuring would it look if the security team was freaking out and losing their shit?"

Chelsea treated me with a grin. "I suppose you have a point." She took a deep breath. "Ready to blow off some steam?"

a small grin tugged at the corner of my mouth. "Lead the way."

After greeting the bouncer, who gave me a long, appraising look, Chelsea led my inside and straight to the bar. I'd been hoping for a booth or something a bit more private, but I wasn't going to complain. When we sat down, she introduced me to her friend June.

Recognition sparked in her eyes when she looked at me again. "Wait. You're the wreath guy!"

I smirked. *Interesting nickname.* "I...yes?"

June nodded appreciatively. "My girl here hasn't stopped talking about how much she loves it. I mean, not going to argue with her. It's gorgeous. But with how she goes on about it, you'd think there was more to it than just appreciation for an evergreen decoration." She winked at Chelsea.

"I haven't talked non-stop about it."

A quick glance at Chelsea had me full-on smiling. The flustered expression mixed with red all over her cheeks was completely adorable. *If a simple wreath impressed her this much...*

I mentally promised to do whatever I could to make that happen as much as possible.

June could only chat a little before heading off. She was one of the bartenders working, which gave me and Chelsea more alone time together. I thought we would have talked more, but we fell into a comfortable silence and sipped on our drinks. There was music playing, and I noticed some people dancing on a nearby makeshift dance floor. When a slower song came on, a far-away look filled her eyes as she smiled.

"Good memory?"

Chelsea blinked and focused on me. "I just love this song. It's always puts a smile on my face."

I held my hand out. "Dance with me."

"What?" Her mouth dropped open in disbelief.

I took her hand in mine, led her out to the dance floor, and wrapped my arms around her waist, pulling her closer to me. As we swayed to the music, her hands slowly slid up my arms, sending warm tingles through me as they settled on the back of my neck. I let out a sigh at the contact and her gaze lifted to meet mine.

As I leaned down and rested my head against Chelsea's, I couldn't help but whisper the lyrics of the song to her. The heated look in her eyes warmed my soul like nothing else ever had. Staring into those eyes, I couldn't hold back anymore, I took her lips in a kiss that had us both moving closer. When she was fully against me, my hardness pressed against her stomach and she pulled herself a little closer, letting out a soft chuckle.

This woman is going to be the death of me.

When we broke the kiss, she whispered something, but I was still reeling from the kiss to process her words. I took a deep breath in an attempt to get a hold of myself, realizing just how lost in her I was. I opened my mouth to say things I never thought I'd say in my life, but snapped my mouth shut before the words could escape. Maybe it was everything that had happened, but I felt closer to her than our time together should have allowed, and that was a bit overwhelming. "Chels, this... I want..." I let out a frustrated breath.

The lust in her eyes told me exactly what she was thinking, which was awfully close to what I had been about to say. She nodded and whispered, "I know. One day at a time, hotshot. Wouldn't want you to lose your load too quickly."

A chuckle came out. "As soon as you're up for it, I'll show you *just* how long I can go."

She leaned forward and kissed me quickly. "Soon." There was something in the way she said that, combined with the desire in her gaze, that had my knees a bit weak. "Very soon."

The song changed to something faster, and while the spell wasn't broken, the heat between us diminished slightly. June glanced over as Chelsea and I sat down again, studying me. It didn't take a rocket scientist to know she was sizing me up to decide if I was good enough for her best friend.

Am I? I hope so.

Chapter Eleven

Chelsea

Sleep hadn't come easily last night once I finally made it home. I kept replaying the unexpected kiss on the dance floor at the bar... and the kiss goodnight in the parking lot after the wedding rehearsal was done. Phil was becoming more important to me, and I couldn't help but wonder how important I was to him. *I need to get my shit together.*

I was at the lodge bright and early, making sure everything was ready and that Quinn didn't overdo it or lose her mind. The florist arrived on time, and I was in the process of adding the fresh flowers to the centerpieces when Quinn poked her head into the ballroom. "Lianne's coming down in a few. Can you make sure the Reading Room is cleared out?"

Nodding, I finished the centerpiece I'd been working on and headed out.

Peter turned my way when I walked into the lobby "Ben's with his moms, so you won't have to worry about him seeing Lianne."

"Thank you." I gave him a grateful smile as I hurried into the Reading Room. *Thank God it's empty.* Taking a look around the room, I let out a relieved breath when I saw everything perfectly in its place and photo ready.

Lianne was radiant when she walked out of the elevator and into the Reading Room in her knee-length dress. It was sparkly, flirty, and sweet all at the same time. Even with how little I knew the woman, the dress suited her.

I want a less beaded version of that as a date night dress.

"You'd look amazing in it, too."

Phil's sudden appearance made me jump. "You have *got* to stop sneaking up on me, especially when I'm apparently thinking out loud."

He kissed the side of my neck, just below my ear. "I'll think about it."

When I turned around to give him a playful slap for flustering me at work, he was already heading toward the door, probably to patrol something. Just before he walked outside, he glanced over his shoulder and winked at me. I tried really hard to ignore how my heart fluttered at the exchange, but I couldn't.

"Please tell me you two are a thing, because that was one of the most damn adorable things ever."

I jumped and turned around to see Jess, Lianne's best friend and Maid of Honor grinning at me. *I need to stop being so easy to distract and sneak up on.* "Um... I... I don't know."

She rolled her eyes. "These men are something else. For what it's worth, he's totally smitten with you. It's not an act."

Before I had to come up with a response, Lianne called her best friend over, and I took the opportunity to walk out of the Reading Room, closing the doors behind me. Moments later, Quinn came out of the ballroom and tapped her wrist.

It was time.

While I stayed in the wings during the day, so to speak, acting as Quinn's assistant, there were times I had to remind her that she also had family obligations to attend to. One of them being photos.

Julia, Ben's six-year-old niece, was a godsend when she wandered over toward us after the ceremony. "Auntie Kin, can you take a picture with me and Princess Auntie Li and Uncle Ben Ben? Pretty please?"

I smirked and looked at Quinn. "How can you say no to that?"

She sighed and gave the adorable little girl a big grin as she reached out for her hand. "I'd love to take a picture with you."

The look on Lukas's face as he watched the duo walk across the room had me grinning. Nothing could have torn his gaze from Quinn in that moment. *That looks like a man in love if I've ever seen one. It's only a matter of time before he's the one proposing... if Quinn doesn't beat him to it.* Glancing around the room, I couldn't help but smile. Despite the chaos of less than forty-eight hours ago, the amount of friends and family celebrating in the room was nothing short of amazing.

Phil

While most of the individuals involved with Quinn and Lukas's abduction were no longer an issue, there were two who got away. Two people associated with Jeffery we couldn't find. Even with the extra coverage with Mr. Agosti's guys, everyone was still on high alert and probably would continue to be while the Agostis were on site.

Ryan had been scouring hours of surveillance video trying to find more clues as to where they went, but with Justin leaking all kinds of information, the two missing men had been able to skirt the outer limits of all the cameras. We didn't think they would be dumb enough to come back here, especially with all of us watching for anything out of the ordinary, but that didn't mean we were taking any chances, either.

For the wedding day, I had been assigned to patrol both entrances, lobby, and the Reading Room with Gage. I wasn't sure if it was the luck of the draw or someone doing me a favor, but I loved that I got to stay closer to where Chelsea was running around. A smirk appeared on my face as I thought about how I'd been able to sneak up on her and give her a quick kiss without too many people noticing.

From what I saw and heard, the ceremony went off without a hitch, and everything had gone according to plan. Mrs. Agosti had insisted we all take turns coming into the ballroom to sit down and eat a proper dinner, and while it wasn't part of the original plan, none of us were stupid enough to argue with the woman who married the man calling the shots. And if I was being honest with myself, we all were pretty sure she was the one actually in charge today.

Once the cake had been cut and the dancing had begun, Peter came outside and found me. "Lianne told me to give you a fifteen minute break. She also told Quinn she's done working for the night." He glanced over at the ballroom door. "Chelsea is to the left when you walk in, leaning against the wall near the south door."

A grin tugged at the corner of my mouth as anticipation of spending time with Chelsea grew inside me. "Gage still over there?"

"Yep. He's been keeping an eye on her for you, too."

What? "For me?"

Peter shook his head, and a quiet chuckle shook his shoulders. "It's no secret to anyone you have a soft spot for her. We're making sure she stays safe, too."

"Oh. Thanks." I wasn't sure how else to respond, but I loved that the team was looking out for her safety, too.

He gave me a playful shove. "Go enjoy your fifteen."

I headed into the ballroom, nodding at Connor and Maddox as I entered the space. Immediately looking left, I smiled when Chelsea was standing exactly where Peter said. There was a dreamy expression on her face as she looked out over the room at the reception in full swing. When I followed the direction of her gaze, I saw the reason. Lianne and Ben were wrapped up in each other's arms, gently swaying to the music, and Lukas and Quinn were not too far away from them at the edge of the dance floor doing the same. And by how they were looking at each other, they were also lost in their own little world.

I closed the distance between Chelsea and me, and leaned against the wall next to her. "They look really happy. Both couples do. You and Quinn did an amazing job today."

She jumped as soon as I started speaking and stood up straight, but then let out a huff when she glanced over and saw me. "You scared the shit out of me. *Again*. I'm convinced I've lost my touch."

"Sorry. I thought you saw me coming." I slid my arm around her waist, gently pulling her closer to me. "And you *definitely* aren't losing your touch."

Chelsea chuckled and shook her head as her cheeks went pink. "I wish I would have seen you walk in. You make quite the pretty picture all dressed up like that." There was heat in her words and a flicker of lust in her eyes as her attention swept over me.

"Are you flirting with me?"

"You do it often enough, like earlier in the Reading Room before the ceremony. Jess saw you, you know." She glanced around the room, checking for something before returning her attention to me. "Not that I don't want to spend time with you, but aren't you supposed to be working right now?"

I smirked. "Like I keep telling you, I don't work all the time."

When she arched an eyebrow and shot an incredulous look my way, I gestured to the dance floor. "Lianne, via Peter, told me to take a break, and I want to spend it with you. Unless you'd rather *not* spend time with me?"

She clasped her hand around mine and gave me a playful glare. "Quit fishing for an invitation. I'd love to spend time with you, and you know it."

"Then come with me." Giving her hand an extra squeeze, I led her from the ballroom, ignoring the guys in the lobby as I walked past them again.

"Where are we going?"

"My room." *Please like this surprise.*

Unknown to Chelsea, I'd been decorating the hotel room Peter and I had been living in. I'd brought in a small pre-lit Christmas tree, extra strings of lights, and even garland. Peter had given me some crap about it initially, but stopped after he figured out why I was doing it.

I'd barely gotten the door open, and had just flipped on the bathroom light switch, when Chelsea gasped. "What did you do?"

"I decorated."

She elbowed me playfully. "Well, yeah. I see that, but... I... When?"

A grin tugged at my lips. "How many times do I have to tell you I don't work all day every day and actually *do* have a life outside of work?" I walked over to a power strip on the bedside table and turned it on. Chelsea gasped again, making me chuckle.

"This is... amazing."

The Christmas tree was on the table next to the sitting chair, I had draped lights and garland across the window, and lined the top of the walls with white twinkle lights. The joy and delight in her eyes was overwhelming, and I turned Chelsea to face me, pulling her into my arms. "Did you see what else I decorated with?"

Glancing up, a knowing grin appeared on her face when she spotted the mistletoe hanging just below the smoke detector. "Any reason you added that in here?"

I pulled her closer, resting my forehead on hers. "Wishful thinking."

Chelsea lifted her arms and looped them around my neck, pulling our faces closer together. "If you wanted to kiss me, all you had to do was ask."

Before I could respond, her lips pressed to mine and all other coherent thoughts left my mind. Leaning down slightly, I deepened the kiss while pulling her as tight to my chest as I could. She was heaven in my arms. Soft and strong, confident and caring, Chelsea really was everything I wanted in a partner.

It wasn't insignificant that she was a badass that could tackle and throw hands without hesitation. Shit, that was hot as hell and made me like and respect her even more.

Breaking the kiss so we could both breathe, I slowly peppered a line of kisses along her jaw and down her neck. A quiet moan slipped out of her, and I carefully backed up until the back of my legs bumped into the end of the bed. I sat down, gently pulling Chelsea onto my lap at the same time.

She snuggled her head into the spot just about my collarbone, letting out a content sigh. "As much as I love kissing you, can we cuddle for a minute?"

"Of course. Is everything okay?" The one of her voice as she made her request had me a little concerned.

"Yeah, I... I just really like how it feels when you hold me. I feel safe. It's... it's really nice."

Without hesitating, I shifted so we were lying on our sides on the bed and wrapped my arms around her a little tighter. I could tell from the tension in her body there was a lot more she wasn't saying, but I wasn't going to push it. A smile tugged at my lips as I rested my head on top of hers. "I love a good cuddle. We can lay here as long as you want."

Honestly, I wasn't even upset she'd stopped the kissing. Spending the evening with her last night had me feeling a lot, quickly, and it was reassuring to have her just want me to hold her. Providing her comfort in any form soothed me and proved that what was happening between us wasn't just lust. There were worse things than cuddling, and I was delighted to have any time alone with her I could. I knew I came off as the flirt who always wanted to jump into bed with a pretty woman. Many people assumed I was the playboy that had women constantly hanging off me, but if given the choice between going out to a bar or club or staying home, I wanted to be home watching a good show or movie, every single time.

Chelsea snuggled into me a little more. "Thank you."

We sat there in comfortable silence for several minutes, holding each other. When she gently scratched my back, I let out a content moan. "I'll give you about a half hour to stop that."

She snickered and scratched a little harder. "You only have a few minutes of your break left."

"Don't remind me." I nuzzled my face into her hair, loving how good she smelled.

The beautiful woman in my arms shook her head. "You know we can hang out when neither of us are working. We've done it before."

"True. And with all the wedding festivities just about over, there's a better chance of being able to take a breath and do just that."

Chelsea lifted her chin and looked up at me, hope shining in her eyes. "Promise?"

I nodded. "I need more cuddling in my life. Particularly with you."

"Same." After letting out a deep sigh, she untangled her arms from around me and sat up. "I should probably make sure my hair doesn't look unprofessional before I head out."

"I didn't do anything to mess up your hair."

A wide smile appeared on her face as she stood in front of the full-length mirror next to the bathroom door. "While that is true, even snuggling can mess up hair."

"Fair enough. When are you done tonight?"

"Soon, I think. I need to check in with Frank when I get back down there. We are trying to convince Quinn not to work tomorrow. Lukas is in on the plan, so the odds are better. I'm hoping the man is smart enough to be able to keep her in bed for the day."

I tried to cough over my stunned laugh.

Chelsea's eyes went wide as she turned to look at me. "That's *not* how I meant for it to come out... but if that's what works." She shrugged.

Must. Change. The. Topic.

I took a deep breath and let it out slowly. "Let me know when you're heading out. I can walk you to your car."

She chuckled nervously. "You want to walk me to my car?"

A wide grin appeared on my face. "I do. Is that okay?"

Chelsea's cheeks flushed. "Well, yeah. Do you think you'll be able to get away?"

By this time, I was standing in front of her, and our faces were so close, our noses were nearly touching. "I can get away for a few minutes to make sure you're safe."

She closed the distance between us and gave me a gentle kiss. "Good to know. Now, we should probably get out of here before we don't."

"You did just fix your hair, after all."

Chelsea snickered. "Yeah, because *that* was my biggest concern."

Joining in her laughter, I kissed her forehead and took her hand in mine, lacing our fingers together. "Let's go."

After turning off the lights, we walked out of my room and back toward the ballroom where the reception was still in full swing. When I started to pull my hand from hers, she tightened her grasp. "You better be around later."

A smile spread across my face. "Try and stop me."

Chelsea nodded, grinning back at me. "Never." With a wink, she kissed my hand, let go, and wandered back into the ballroom.

Seconds later, a soft chuckle came from behind me. "This is a first. I don't think I've ever seen *you* stunned after talking to a woman."

I rolled my eyes and glanced over to see Peter next to me. "Oh, shut up."

"No snappy comeback? Has the flirting master been bested?"

Without a word, I flipped him off, turned, and walked past him, returning to where I had been stationed before my break. It wasn't that I had been bested, it was that I had been surprised by her response.

Regardless, it was something that didn't happen often, and I freaking loved it.

Chapter Twelve

Chelsea

True to his word, Phil had been waiting for me in the lobby after I was done with my wedding duties and walked me to my car. After a long hug and another heart-stopping kiss, I finally got into my car and drove home.

I fell asleep immediately after changing into pajamas and crawling into bed. I had the best dreams, and even though I didn't want to wake up or get out of bed in the morning, knowing I'd see Phil made it a little easier to leave the warmth and coziness.

Frank had mentioned that Edith was going to make sure there would be a special treat for me in the morning. How could I complain about that? Even the hope of eating one of her famous cinnamon rolls finally got me all the way out the door.

I couldn't help the grin on my face when I pulled into my usual parking place. Phil, who had been standing at the entrance to the lodge, was now making his way toward me and my car. He was next to me by the time I stepped out of my car and closed the door. I shook my head. "Do you ever stop working?"

"I'm not working right now."

I tipped my head to the side. "Then why are you out here?"

"Can't a guy just want to make sure the people important to him are safe?"

My face grew warm, and I pulled my purse closer to me. "I suppose you can."

"Let's go, then."

Phil walked me into the lodge and past the front desk, both of us waving at Damien as we walked through the lobby and toward the ballroom. I was happy Avery was working the front desk later on today instead of me. The insanity of the week had caught up with me, and I needed a break. Taking a deep breath, I pushed open the doors and walked into the ballroom.

Please don't let Quinn be in here.

I let out a sigh when I walked into a blissfully empty room. The kitchen and catering staff had taken care of all the dishes, flatware, and napkins the night before, and Quinn had already gathered all the centerpieces onto one table before Lukas took her home. Everything else was still very much how I left it the night before.

"Need help with anything?"

My heart fluttered slightly as I glanced over at Phil. "Not at the moment. Honestly, and don't take this wrong, but I think you're going to be more of a distraction at this point."

He nodded and gave me a knowing smile. "No offense taken at all. I'm going to check in with Borce and the guys. You'll let me know if you need anything, yeah?"

I waved my phone at him. "I promise."

After one last hug, Phil left, and I took a moment to make a game plan for the morning. While it didn't take me long to gather all the table linens and put them in the rolling bin to be washed, it did take me a little longer to pack up the centerpieces and put them away.

Miles strolled in about the time I headed toward one of the storage closets to start bringing out more tables. "I know you are more than capable of handling this, but please let me help you with something."

Grinning, I nodded. "There's a wedding shower this afternoon, and I need four more round tables and eight chairs to go around each one of them."

"I'll get started on that if you want to move onto the next thing on your checklist."

Deciding I needed more coffee before tackling the linens and re-dressing the tables, I headed to the kitchen.

Edith glanced over as I walked in. "Please tell me you haven't seen Quinn this morning?"

I shook my head. "Nope. I thought Frank told her to take the day off."

My wonderful work mom and boss rolled her eyes. "Even *that* doesn't stop everyone."

Frank sauntered into the kitchen and kissed his wife on the cheek. "What's this I'm hearing my name about?"

Edith chuckled. "Chelsea and I were talking about how hard it is to get Quinn to take a few days off. I know she still feels guilty about the drama that followed her here."

Frank let out a deep sigh. "I know she does, and while I can't change how she feels about the drama, that really isn't her fault, but I can keep reminding her that we appreciate her all the same."

Before I could weigh in, Phil walked in. "Hey, Edith. Any chance I can get a brunch basket?"

The man looked hot in his dark blue jeans and dark green button-down shirt, and I had to close my mouth before I started drooling. *Get it together, woman. You saw him earlier. He hasn't changed.*

Edith turned toward him and smiled. "You could have called it in, dear. You didn't have to walk down here."

Phil nodded. "Oh, I know. I want to deliver it to Lukas and

Quinn before they have a chance to wander over themselves... as a way to encourage them not to leave the cabin."

"So you're on our side, I see."

He looked my way, tipping his head to the side. "Your side of *what?*"

Edith patted his shoulder. "Getting Quinn... well, her *and* Lukas, to take a few days off and just be. But to answer your question, I'll happily put a basket together for them."

He grinned. "That? Oh, I'm one hundred percent on your side. If anyone needs a couple days away, it's Quinn and with Lukas next to her. I think he's going to try convincing her to extend her time off today, but I don't know how successful he's going to be."

"Time to pull out the big guns, I see." I winced. "Sorry... terrible word choice. All I meant was that we might need to call in a favor."

Phil arched an eyebrow in intrigue. "Who or what do you know that I don't?"

I shook my head, snickering. *He thinks he's so smart.* "Have any of you thought of asking Ben and Lianne for their help? I know they just got married, but desperate times call for desperate measures. Quinn is related to Ben and also feels indebted to Lianne for saving hers and Lukas's lives. Pretty significant, if you ask me. Besides, we all know Quinn will listen to them and give way less pushback than if it came from any of us."

"She's got a point." Frank nodded as he leaned against the wall.

Chuckling, I turned to Edith. "Any chance you can whip up some cookies or pastries for the lovebirds? I think personally delivered sugary bribes are in order. I even volunteer to deliver it. Lianne is least likely to yell at me, and she and I have already talked about how Quinn needs time off."

Phil

Between the baskets of treats delivered to the respective people and several phone calls and text conversations, Lukas and Quinn confirmed they would be taking several days off.

Not long after, a message came in through our group chat.

Lukas: < I want to take Quinn to the house in a few days. Can you all make sure there's enough set up that it can at least pass as a rental? >

Ryan: < Is that the story you're feeding her? >

Lukas: < Until I bring her there, yes. >

Lukas: < Don't worry, Lianne has already made me aware of her opinions on the topic. >

I chuckled as I typed out my response.

Phil: < I'll check in on it today and see what I can do. >

Lukas: < Do you think Chelsea would be willing to help out? Quinn loves how she decorates things. >

Phil: < I'll ask her, but I'm pretty sure she'll be up for it. >

Checking the time, I sent out a text before running out of the room.

Phil: < are you still on property? >

I slid on my shoes while waiting for her reply. A ding from my phone brought a smile to my face.

Chelsea: < I was just wrapping up set up with Edith. What's up? >

Phil: < Can we chat before you leave? I have a favor to ask you. >

Chelsea: < Oh damn. A favor? You never ask for

those. I feel there's a story behind that. Okay. Yeah. I'll text you when I'm done. >

An hour later there was a soft knock on my door. Intrigued, I got off the couch from where I had been reading, immediately throwing open the door after I glanced through the peephole. "Hey!"

A sheepish but pleased grin was on Chelsea's face. "I know I said I'd text, but I figured there was no harm in stopping by here first."

I pulled her in for a tight hug. "I love that you did. Now, how much buttering up do I need to do before asking you my favor."

She chuckled. "Have you had lunch yet? Because I could go for some food."

"Are you free for the rest of the day?"

"I am. Why?"

Here goes something. "If I take you out to eat, you'll do me a favor? Well, it's actually more a favor for Lukas, but will benefit Quinn."

Chelsea slid her hand into mine. "You had me five words in. Let's go."

A grin slid across my face when I figured it out. "Dot's Diner work for you?"

"Always. I freaking love that place."

After driving there and ordering our food, I filled in Chelsea on what Lukas needed from us. She was immediately on board.

Chelsea

After we were done eating, Phil drove us over to the house. My jaw dropped as we rolled up the long driveway. "Holy crap. This is gorgeous!" A modern wood and steel clad ranch sat in an open cove, flanked by spruce trees, overlooking an open field. I stepped out of the car and stood there, openly staring at it. "I didn't even know this house was here!"

Phil chuckled. "I think this is a case of Lukas knew a guy."

I shook my head. "Of course he did. Well, where to first?"

"Connor told me all the deliveries are in the garage. Do you want to dive into unpacking them, or would you rather have the tour first?"

"I'm all about working smarter. We can bring in some of the boxes and go from there."

He slid his hand into mine. "Let's get it started, then."

I was not prepared for the mountain of boxes waiting for us in the garage. Yes, Phil had told me what all Lukas had ordered, but seeing it all in front of me was a little overwhelming. *This is for Quinn. If anyone deserves it, it's her.* Once we started bringing in boxes, we kept going until they were all lined up in rows in the empty living room. Glancing around, I couldn't stop the question. "Lukas *did* order furniture for this place, right?"

Phil nodded. "Oh yeah. I think it's getting delivered tomorrow, so anything we don't unpack tonight needs to get moved out of there."

"Challenge accepted."

Over the next several hours, Phil and I opened, unpacked, and sorted out the content of dozens of boxes. As soon as the kitchen basics appeared, I started filling the kitchen sink with water, grateful for the soup we found in one of the first boxes. I washed and dried, and once all the boxes were open, Phil helped me figure out where to put things.

"If Quinn or Lukas hates it, it's on them to change it."

It was hard not to watch him while I worked. Seeing Phil in such a domestic setting somehow made him hotter, especially when he set up a little area at the end of the counter and assembled two lamps for side tables yet to be delivered. *I'd love to spend more time with him like this.*

He caught me staring at me, and smirked before shaking his head. "You're making it hard for me to stay on task, Chels."

"Sounds more like your problem than mine." I winked at him and took the opportunity to grab a full garbage bag and take it out to the garage. As much as I wanted to wrap myself around that man and do more than one indecent thing to him, doing those things in his boss and my co-worker's house felt wrong. Removing myself from the room he was in seemed like a good plan to give myself a moment to settle down and clear my mind.

It had been a good plan until I heard the door leading from the house to the garage open.

"You okay?"

I turned and nodded. "Yep. Just taking a minute to cool off."

"Is the house too warm? I can turn down the thermostat."

How do I tell him I'm trying not to jump him? "It's not that. I'm... I'm trying to behave myself. You're a very cute boy." I winked at him.

Phil chuckled and ran his hand through his hair. "I see. Well, if we're being honest, you're a very cute girl who is also making it hard to behave." He gave me a knowing look. The lust in his eyes probably matched my own.

I reached out and gave his hand a squeeze. "I'll only be another minute or two. Don't you worry about me."

"Now *that* I can't promise."

I let out an amused chuckle as I watched him walk back into the house. "No, I suppose you can't."

The rest of the evening went without incident. I washed and dried towels and curtains, and once I ironed the curtains, I hung them on the curtain rods Phil had just installed in the living room when my stomach let out a growl. "Any chance there's food in one of those boxes?"

Phil shook his head. "No. Want to go out or order in?"

I flopped onto the one chair in the corner. "I feel sweaty and gross and don't want to be social with other people right now. ."

"Want to eat here or back in my room where there is actual furniture to sit on?"

"Let's go back to the lodge." I looked around. "Will you be coming back tomorrow?"

Phil nodded. "Yep."

"You want my help again?"

He gave me a surprised look. "If you want to. I don't want to assume you don't have more exciting plans on a Sunday."

I let out a loud laugh. "Listen, I know the tight deadline you all are up against. I can spare a few hours to make sure the grand surprise is ready for Monday."

Chapter Thirteen

Chelsea

We worked all day on Sunday, frantically decorating and adding finishing touches, but by dinner time, the house was ready for Lukas and Quinn, and we were not disappointed by the reaction. Ryan, still grateful that I had brought his favorite donuts and helped them with the house, invited me and Phil to see the look on Quinn's face.

I hadn't realized how many cameras he'd installed, and before I could make an argument about invading their privacy, he promised to cut off our access to the feed once we saw her reaction, or if things took a sudden steamy turn.

"You'd be shocked by some of the things I've seen on camera. Trust me. I Know when to turn off the screen." The slightly haunted look in Ryan's eyes told me he wasn't kidding.

The only downside of the house being done was it meant Phil was moving out of the lodge. He promised I'd still see him all the time, and he made a point to still be at the entrance when I pulled up for work on Tuesday morning, but there was still a little part of me that was sad he was farther away.

Will things change between us now?

I was sitting in the kitchen, trying to distract myself with lunch, when my phone buzzed.

June: < Have things settled down enough that you can have a night out with me? >

Chelsea: < Yes. And PLEASE! I've been missing you. When can we go out? >

June: < Tomorrow? I'm actually off. >

Chelsea: < Done. I get off work at 4:30pm. Meet me at my house at 5? We can get ready and then head over. >

June. < Done. >

The rest of the day and following flew by, and the next thing I knew, I was pulling into my driveway and hurrying into my house.

Time to transform into a knockout.

A few minutes later there was a knock, immediately followed by the sound of my front door opening. "Hellooo!" My best friend's voice traveled upstairs to where I was in my bedroom.

"I'm up here." I was standing in front of my closet in the middle of changing from my professional clothes to something far more bar appropriate. So far I had swapped out my pencil skirt for pleather pants. I was still debating between a leather and lace long-sleeved corset-looking bodysuit and a tight V-neck shirt.

June appeared in my doorway wearing a vintage rock tee that was cut in a fun way to show off some of the large angel wings tattooed on her back, black lace-up pants, combat boots, and had a leather jacket draped over her arm. "Please tell me you are not wearing that button-down shirt tonight."

I chuckled and shook my head. "No. I just haven't decided which top to change into."

"The bodysuit, obviously. Your boobs look fantastic in it. Besides, maybe that hottie you introduced me to will see you in it and really get things heated up."

My face grew warm as I thought of what Phil's reaction would be. *Should I send him a picture and ask what he thinks?*

As I headed toward the bathroom to do the necessary gymnastics to get into said bodysuit, June let out a sigh. "I still can't believe we are going to the bar on my night off."

"Neither of us wanted to drive into the city or go to the biker bar tonight. And *you* were the one insisting we needed to go out for our girls' night."

"Yeah, yeah, yeah. Hurry up so we can get there. You can buy me a drink for your troubles."

"Hey, Dennis."

The older gentleman at the door nodded at us and smiled as we walked up from where June had parked. "Good evening, Ladies. June, I'm a little surprised to see you here on your night off."

She rolled her eyes and gestured at me. "I had to get in a girl's night out with my best friend, and this, of course, was the best option."

I waved at him. "I also wanted to see my favorite bouncer."

Dennis chuckled. "I'm flattered, even if I think you're making up stories. Word on the street is you have one certain security guard you might rank a little higher than me these days. I'm surprised he isn't here tonight."

I shot a glare at my best friend. "Really?"

June shrugged. "What? Tell me I'm wrong, especially with how cozy you two were the other night."

Before I could launch into a tirade, Dennis patted my arm. "Take it easy on her. All she said to me was there was a good-looking security guard who had caught your eye. I hope he treats you well and respects you like you deserve."

Taking a deep breath and letting it out slowly, I nodded. "You make a good point, and he does."

With a nod, he waved us into the building. Upon entering, we made our way to the far end of the bar, our favorite place to sit. As soon as we settled onto our stools, one of the bartenders, Reece, came over.

"June, Chelsea, what can I get you tonight?"

June leaned forward, resting an elbow on the edge of the bar. "Hey, Reece, two red-headed sluts and vodka cranberries, please."

He nodded, shaking his head in amusement. "Coming right up."

As he walked away, my best friend shifted to face me. "So, Phil's importance has increased, I see. A week ago you brought him in to blow off some steam and ended up on the dance floor cheek to cheek. I know you well enough to know there's more to the story. Care to fill in your bestie?"

I gulped. *Here we go.* "Can I get some alcohol in me first?"

June's eyes went wide as she let out a low whistle. "Oh, shit. You fell for him. You fell hard, too."

"I..." I trailed off, unable to finish the sentence. *Have I fallen for him? Of course I have. Only an idiot would say otherwise.* "I didn't mean to." The words barely came out as a whisper.

Her hand rested on my back and rubbed it gently. "But he made it impossible not to?"

I nodded, memories from the past few weeks flickered through my mind. "Yeah, something like that."

As Reece set our drinks in front of us and quietly slid away, giving us privacy, a twinkle appeared in June's eyes. "It's not a bad thing, I swear. I'm just excited you've finally found someone worthy of your time and attention. I know how few worthy guys there are in this town."

"True."

"To good men!" June held her shot glass up and I tapped mine against her.

"To good men." I'd barely taken a sip of my vodka cranberry when the scent of cheap cologne slammed into me. A quick glance at June told me she'd caught a whiff of it as well. Her eyes locked on something behind me, and the new twinkle in her eyes confirmed there was at least someone good-looking to accompany the smell.

"Ladies, can we join you?"

We? I glanced over my shoulder and saw two guys standing behind us. One I didn't know, but the other guy looked familiar. *Wait. No. That can't be who I think it is.*

"Of course you can."

My eyes widened a little at June's response. It wasn't like her to add guys to a girls' night, especially when she begged for me to come out, but the guy I didn't recognize was *exactly* her type, and not someone I'd ever seen around here, either. I was not about to cock block my best friend, even if the guy he was with was who I thought he was. Nothing but trouble.

"I'm Garrison."

June's smile grew as she took in the hottie in front of her. "I'm June. It's a pleasure to meet you."

Garrison took her hand in his and kissed her knuckles. "The pleasure is all mine."

I was almost impressed. *Almost.* The man he was friends with had my intuition screaming that something was off, but I decided to play it cool. At least for now.

The friend moved his attention to me. "Since my best friend is enamored with your best friend, I'm Sylas."

It is him! Ugh. I gave him my best smile, trying not to broadcast that I knew *exactly* who he was. "I'm Chelsea."

His face lit up with confused recognition. "You seem familiar. Have we met before?"

"Nope. I'm sure I would have remembered meeting you." It wasn't a lie. We'd never been formally introduced. I just knew from friends and acquaintances who he was and who he was related to.

"I know without a doubt I would have remembered meeting you before tonight. I know *my* night definitely just improved. You're a knockout." My skin crawled as he raked over my body with his gaze

I flicked my attention toward June, who was already deep into a flirtatious conversation with Garrison, and let out a tiny groan. *This is going to be a long night.*

"I hope to be hearing *a lot* more of that later on tonight."

Gross, dude. I somehow suppressed a shudder and took a large sip of my drink. "That's going to be a hard pass, sorry."

"I guess we'll have to see how persuasive I can be."

I took another sip of my drink, willing the bartender to come over so I could order another. *What I'd give to have Phil here.* After I set my glass down, I put on my best 'customer service smile.' "So, what were your plans tonight before running into us?"

Sylas took my question as an invitation to move closer to me. "Well, Garrison came into town to visit me. It's been years since we've hung out, and I wanted to kick off the night with a few drinks."

I can work with this. "I wouldn't want June and I to interrupt guy's night. We should let you two catch up."

Sylas's eyes twinkled with amusement and something that made the hairs on the back of my neck stand on end. "The only thing you two are guilty of are adding some much needed *entertainment*, if you will."

"Can we get your next round?"

June glanced at Garrison, who had posed the question to me, then smirked before responding. "Sure."

I knew that smirk. She was about to see what this guy was about, and how much he was going to shell out for drinks before we headed out. Well, that was what the smirk *usually* meant. The way she was staring at this guy, there was a tiny chance she might be making out or sleeping with the guy before the night was over.

Am I walking home tonight?

"I need to use the lady's room. I'll be right back." Without waiting for a response, I hopped off the barstool and made my way to the bathroom.

The door was barely shut behind me when it was shoved open again. "What's wrong?"

I took a deep breath and let it out slowly as I ran my hands over my hair and tightened my ponytail. "Nothing."

June arched her eyebrow. "Want to try that again and *not* lie this time?"

I paced back and forth in the small space for a moment. "Ugh, fine. You know how shit went down at work?" When June nodded, I went on. "Well, Sylas is related to one of the guys who was causing a lot of the trouble." I shook off the memory of chasing after Justin and tackling him to the ground.

"Okay." She studied my face. "What else?"

Resting my hands on the sink, I took a deep breath. "You didn't hear this, but I was involved with his capture, and I don't know if Sylas knows that or not."

"Oh, shit."

I nodded. "Yeah."

"Do you think he's attached to what happened?"

"That's the thing. I have no idea. I didn't think his cousin was capable of pulling what he did, but he proved us all wrong there."

My best friend studied my face and then nodded slowly. "So which of us is going to be sick? You should probably be the one, since you went running in here first."

"What?" That was not the response I'd been expecting.

June huffed out a sigh. "I don't want to force you to hang out with someone who makes you uncomfortable. I figured you 'getting sick' would be the fastest way to get us out of here if you want to leave."

"What? June. No. First, Garrison seems nice enough, even if his choice of friends is questionable. Second, I don't want to ruin our night. Third, no one runs *us* out of *your* bar. That's not how things work here."

She walked forward and poked me in the chest. "While all that may be true, no man is worth making my best friend horribly uncomfortable."

I shook my head. "It could be fine. It's just a drink and some conversation. Besides, if they get too out of line, I know you'll have them removed."

My best friend stared into my eyes again, as if she was searching for a lie. "Fine. I can live with this plan. Dennis could probably use some entertainment tonight. It's been pretty quiet here lately."

There was no stopping the gasp that came out of me. "June! You *never* say the Q word, *especially* in retail, hospitality, or medical places. It's the kiss of death and you know it."

She snickered. "I phrased it carefully. Regardless, are you good to head back out?"

I took a deep breath and nodded as I released it in a rush. "Yeah."

"And you promise to let me know the second you want to leave?"

"I promise."

June gave me a big smile. "Excellent. Let's go enjoy our free drinks and see if the guys know anything about keeping up a conversation."

When we returned to the bar and June slid onto her bar stool, Garrison scooted closer to her, wrapping an arm around her waist. Sylas tried to do the same thing to me, but I turned and flagged down Reece to avoid the contact. I didn't want any part of Sylas touching me. *Since June is all wrapped up in Garrison, should I text Phil?*

It was a minute before Reece could make his way over, but when he did, he brought two vodka cranberries with him.

"I was waiting for you and June to come back before making and delivering these."

I gave him the most grateful smile. "One of the many reasons you are my favorite bartender, Reece."

Out of the corner of my eye, I saw June shoot me a dirty look. We both knew she was my favorite bartender, but it was fun to tell him he was, too.

Reece smiled and shook his head. "Just doing my job." He glanced up. "Gentlemen, are you still doing okay?"

The guys nodded, and Reece moved onto the next patron vying for his attention.

"So, on a first name basis with the bartender? How often do you two come here?"

If only he knew. A smirk tugged at the corner of my mouth as I answered him. "It's a small town, Sylas. You know there aren't a ton of local options. Also, June and I don't like staying in every night."

A hand landed on the bare skin of my back and traced the edge of the bodysuit, and I immediately tensed up, brushing his hand away and grinding my teeth at his touch.

"Hey. You'd be more than safe with me. I'd never let anything happen to you."

Every hair on the back of my neck stood up. *Why would he say it like that?*

I gave him a fake smile as I shook off the comment and returned my attention to the other two people in our group. Garrison and June did most of the conversational heavy lifting. Sylas chimed in pretty frequently, but I was having a hard time getting chatty. I couldn't shake the uneasy feeling in my stomach. Like Justin, I have never heard anything particularly bad about Sylas, but then I hadn't heard anything good, either.

Even after a couple drinks, I couldn't let myself fully relax. *I don't want to be here anymore. Time to go.* "Well, I have an early morning, so I think I'm going to head out."

Sylas took a step closer to me, brushing a loose hair from my face. I jerked back from his touch. "If you're worried about not getting enough beauty sleep, you don't need to. You're pretty enough to miss an hour or two of sleep. Let me take care of you."

Yeah, that's going to be a hard pass. "Thanks, but I can take care of myself."

June caught the look I threw at her and responded with the tiniest nod before standing up. "She's my ride, so I'm going to be heading out, too."

As if on cue, Garrison put his arm around June's waist and started to pull her closer to him. "Don't feel like you have to rush out. I can always bring you home later if you want to stay. I'd love to spend more time with you."

She turned, politely removing his arm from her. "Maybe another night, if you play your cards right."

He paused for a moment before nodding. "Good thing I'm excellent at cards."

Sylas moved closer to me, putting his hand on my hip. "I'm not giving up as easily as Garrison. All I know about you is that you're a pretty little thing who wishes she had a big, strong man to take care of her. If peace and quiet is what you want, you can always come back to our place. We can *really* get to know each other there without any prying eyes or unwanted interruptions. Trust me when I say it would be a night you wouldn't forget."

Does this really work on other women? A quick glance at June showed me she was as pissed by Sylas's little speech as I was, and I pushed away his hand. "Maybe another time." *Or never.*

He leaned in. "I know what you did to my cousin. The least you can do is have a conversation with me. Wouldn't want someone else to get hurt."

I froze, but tried to cover it by grabbing my glass and taking a drink. *What the hell does he mean by that? Does he know?* I glanced over at June, who had the same wide-eyed expression. *I need to get us out of here without them following.* After taking another sip, I sat up a little straighter and turned to face them, a wide smile on my face. "You're absolutely right. I don't want anyone else to get hurt."

A smug sneer appeared on his lips. "I *knew* you were as smart as you are pretty."

I turned up the charm and batted my eyelashes at him. "And I wish you were half as good-looking as you are stupid and arrogant." I dropped the cutesy act. "Threaten me again. I fucking dare you."

He blinked at me, the arrogance faltering. "What?"

Standing up straighter, I glared up at the idiot before me. "We clearly weren't interested in leaving with you before. You did *not* improve your odds by threatening me, and you *really* don't want to find out what will happen if you don't leave us alone."

Sylas leaned in. "And what could *you* possibly do? Toss your drink in my face? Kick me in the shin? *You're a weak, little girl.* You—"

His word was cut off by a pained squeak as I wrapped my

hand around his dick and squeezed. "I'm going to make what I did to your cousin look like child's play if you can't figure out how to leave us alone. I know the entire story of what happened to Justin. I know how he ran like a bitch when I caught him red-handed. I know how he wasn't able to get away from me after I tackled him. I also know who I left in charge of deciding his fate. I may *only* be some tiny, weak woman to you, but right now I'm the one who has all the power to decide if you spend the night in a hospital or not." I squeezed a little harder, digging my nails in, nearly bringing the man to his knees. "So, what kind of night do you want to have?"

"I'll... leave." The words were barely choked out through the pain.

"Promise?"

When he nodded, I released my vice-like grip. Sylas almost collapsed in relief, but managed to stand with the help of his friend. "Crazy bitch."

Play dumb games, get dumb prizes. I slapped him as hard as I could across the face, collecting even more attention from the rest of the patrons in the bar. "How dare you try to shove your hand down my pants!" I tossed the nearest drink in his face and looked at June, who looked almost as shocked as he did. "Come on, June. Let's get the hell out of here and away from these assholes."

I linked arms with my best friend and all but dragged her out of the bar and to her car.

Please don't follow us. Please don't follow us. Please don't follow us.

I had never been so happy to get both of us into my condo and lock the door in my entire life.

Later that night, after June had left, I finally checked my phone. A message almost immediately popped up.

Phil: < I hope you had a good night. :) >

Shit. I knew if Phil even caught a whiff of what had happened, he'd come in guns blazing.

Would that be so bad?

I needed to talk to Quinn.

Phil

I knew Chelsea was going out with her best friend tonight, and I would have shadowed them, but two things had stopped me. One, she asked me not to, claiming she wanted a night that felt normal. Two, I had to work.

Once I was back at the house after work, I showered, flopped onto my bed, and grabbed my phone, finally giving into my urge to check in with her.

Phil: < I hope you had a good night. :) >

There was only a slight delay before she responded.

Chelsea: < I had a great time with June. >

I didn't like that answer. It was too carefully worded and not like the usual messages from her. *What happened?*

Chelsea: < Hope *you* had a good night. I'm off to bed. See you tomorrow. :) >

Now I was certain something had to have happened. Chelsea loved to fill me in on whatever gossip she overheard when she went out. It took everything for me not to tap into the local surveillance feeds and try to piece it together. *Take a breath. She's probably just tired. If something happened, she'd tell you.*

Chapter Fourteen

Chelsea

I flopped onto one of the wooden chairs surrounding a matching wooden table in the corner of the kitchen and let out an exhausted breath. It had been a crazy morning, and after the semi-disastrous girls night out with my best friend, I was very much over today and the week in general. Not that I was complaining about having 'normal drama.' *Is it normal, though?* I couldn't shake what Sylas had said in the bar last night, and I certainly couldn't stop thinking about how it possibly was connected to the insanity with Quinn, her psycho ex, and the crazy connections of her current boyfriend.

Edith set a steaming bowl in front of me and patted me on the shoulder. "Eat up, sweetie. I've got peanut butter chocolate chip cookie bars almost ready. If you're good, I'll even get some ice cream out."

"You're an angel sent from above." This woman was a saint and the best bonus mom you could ask for, and I was desperate for the comfort of one of her meals.

Her laughter bounced around the kitchen as she returned to

the prep area where Allen, the other chef, and their two assistants were busy chopping and prepping things for dinner.

I'd barely eaten three bites when Quinn strolled in, inhaling deeply. "Chicken and dumplings? Yes!"

I nodded. "*And* Edith's got cookie bars in the oven."

"I thought I smelled peanut butter when I walked in." She strolled over to the stove, grabbed the ladle, and filled a bowl before joining me at the small table. "So, what's going on?"

"Hmm?"

Quinn stared at me like she was trying to figure out a puzzle. "You're not your usual, cheery self today. I thought you'd be floating after your night out with your bestie."

I stabbed at one of the dumplings in my bowl. "I wish I was."

"What happened?"

"Let's just say some guys are complete assholes."

My work bestie set down her spoon, rested her arms on the table, and leaned forward. "Who's ass am I kicking?"

I shook my head. "You don't need to kick anyone's ass... or do anything. He eventually left us alone after I made it abundantly clear it was his best and only option."

"Chelsea..." Quinn stared at me. "What happened?"

Where do I start? "Well, aside from getting way up in my personal space and refusing to keep his hands to himself, he kept saying really misogynistic and douche-y things. Just because I'm 5'2" does not mean I'm weak and need a man around to help me and take care of me." I let out a sigh. "Then there was how he threatened me after I refused to let him take me home and 'get to know him better'."

"Are you kidding me? He *threatened* you? What in the hell could he have possibly threatened you with?"

I took a deep breath and let it out slowly. Quinn was just settling back into a normal life. The last thing I wanted to do was stir up drama with her and Lukas and his guys.

"Chelsea Marie, what did he say to you?"

I stirred my lunch, trying to stay calm. "Just that he knew what I did to his cousin Justin, and that he wouldn't want anyone else to get hurt."

When I glanced up, Quinn's eyes were wide, she looked pale, and her lips were pressed into a tight line. "How did you get away from him?"

"I squeezed his dick and balls until he promised he'd leave us alone."

She snickered and shook her head. "Well, I can't say I don't like your style. Have you told Phil?"

I shook my head. His face flashed through my mind. *Phil would flip if he knew what happened, especially since he was there for the whole Justin tackle. This isn't going to end well.*

"Chelsea! Why not?"

Another deep sigh came out. "He would flip out. Lukas and all his guys would. It's fine. He left me and June alone."

"And what's the plan when he bugs you again?"

"I see you also didn't use the word 'if.' I'll figure something out. Maybe I'll make sure I have someone with me."

My amazing co-worker reached across the table and rubbed my arm. "Even if you take someone with you every single time, it shouldn't have to be like that, Chelsea. You have every right to have a fun night out without being harassed, just like any other patron there. Also, you're taking the grand assumption he's not going to escalate the situation. Look at my life the past few months."

"I know."

"You know we have to tell the guys, right?"

My head popped up. "Please don't take this to Lukas. It's just some stupid guy running his mouth. It will be fine."

Quinn glared at me. "Again, do I need to remind you of all the shit 'just some stupid guy' pulled when I wouldn't take him back?"

I stared at her, noting the still-fading bruising on her cheek. "Okay, fine. Point made. I don't think this is *quite* the same situation, but if you feel like you have to mention this to Lukas, *please* don't make a big deal about it. I have a feeling he'd come in, guns blazing, and that is the last thing we all need right now." *Maybe they will take it better coming from Quinn and not overreact, or will it be worse coming from her? Will Phil be mad I didn't tell him?*

Quinn snickered. "I'm just going to relay the information. I can't control how he's going to react to it. You know how he gets about protecting his family."

I sat up a little straighter, leaning forward and resting my elbows on the table, grateful for something else to focus on that wasn't about me. "*Family*, you say? Is there something I should know?" I glanced at her hands and didn't see any new jewelry, but that didn't necessarily mean anything.

The red all over her face almost negated the glare she shot me. "You know damn well that after everything that went down in that abandoned mining building, the entire family took me in as one of their own. But before you ask, no, there have been no formal declarations or gifts of intent."

"Says the woman living in a house her boyfriend bought with the sole purpose of living closer to her and keeping her safe."

Her blush deepened. "So? We haven't even been together for six months yet."

"And? Sounds like a lame excuse. My parents were engaged six weeks after meeting, and with a fraction of the *bonding experiences* you and Lukas have had. Time is a construct, *ma'am*. Honestly, I'm surprised you haven't proposed to *him* already."

Quinn made a show of busying herself with eating her lunch.

"I thought we were talking about your boy problems, not the jeweled status of my left hand. When are you going to tell Phil?"

I'd been grateful for the distraction, but she was a pro at redirection. "Can you tell him and not Lukas?"

Her mouth dropped open. "Chelsea! He's going to flip out when he finds out, and he's probably going to be a little pissed he's hearing about it from me and not you. You guys are together, aren't you?"

"I... Well... no? I mean..." My heart raced as a slight panic washed over me. "I thought we were being subtle."

Quinn threw her head back in laughter. "Depends on the day and who's nearby. You're always professional when guests are around, but alone?" She fanned herself. "You two could start a fire with some of the looks you give each other. Do I even need to mention the kiss he snuck before the wedding, or how you both disappeared during the reception together?"

Now it was my turn to blush. "We do not start fires. And how did you know about that when you weren't even in the same room."

Quinn stood up, collecting her dirty dishes. "One, I can provide photographic proof if you'd like. Two, I hear things."

My thoughts jumped to Ryan, specifically his comment about the things he'd seen on surveillance cameras. *Shit.*

I glanced toward Edith, who nodded at me. "It's not exactly a secret, my dear. All the guys razz him for it."

"We've always kept things professional." I stuttered out the words, feeling exposed now that I realized everyone I worked with saw through the ruse.

Quinn set her bowl and spoon down, letting out a long breath. "You have overall, and very well, I will add. All I'm saying is Phil would happily help you out if you just asked, but I also know you want more than just *help* from him." With a wink, she scooped up her dishes, and flounced over to where Edith was working on butter-cream for the cookie bars.

She's not wrong about any of it. He'd probably insist on coming with me everywhere, not that I would mind, but it's not the point.

It bothered me how much this was bothering me.

Phil

Today had been a long day, mostly because nothing had happened. It was a blessing and a curse. I wasn't complaining about the lack of insanity, but it had left me a little too much time to think about a certain blond woman behind the front desk, and how she had taken over all my thoughts. I was also frustrated that every time I went to talk to Chelsea, she was busy, and then by the time I finished up a project for Frank, she had left for the day. What made it worse is I hadn't heard a thing from her all day, and Quinn had been acting a little off, too.

Peter and I had eaten dinner and cleaned up, and he was already in his room for the night, something about having a headache and wanting to sleep it off. That actually worked out better for me. I was looking forward to mindlessly watching some TV... and maybe talking to Chelsea

I was about to sit on the couch when there was a knock on the door near the security room, just before it opened and Quinn poked her head in. "Is it okay if I come down and hang out? I don't want to bother you if you're busy or trying to relax or something."

"Sure. Of course. Is everything okay?" I walked over, slightly on edge by the concerned expression on her face.

She nodded. "I'm fine. Do you have a minute to chat, though?"

It wasn't the first time she had come downstairs to hang out with one of us. I knew all too well how lonely an empty house felt.

While I was honored she felt comfortable enough to come to us if she needed something, I knew there was something bigger brewing if she was down here and not on the phone with Lukas. He was out of town for the week, but I knew he would have dropped pretty much anything to take her call. "Come on in and make yourself comfortable. I was just about to make some popcorn. You want any?"

Quinn let out a relieved breath and walked into the room, closing the door behind her. "Thanks, and I'd love some."

While I was in the kitchen pulling things together, Quinn sat on the dining room chair nearest me. "Want anything to drink with the popcorn?"

"Whatever you're pouring."

I nodded and turned toward the fridge, opened it, and took out a can of her favorite pop and a bottle of her favorite wine. Ever since she moved in and started hanging out with me and Peter, we made sure to have a couple of her favorite drinks on hand at all times. While it was our job to keep her safe, we also wanted her to be comfortable hanging out with us, and didn't want her to feel like she had to bring her own snacks.

Quinn shook her head. "You know I have my own wine upstairs, right? You don't have to keep buying it just for when I come down here to hang out."

She's onto us. "I happen to like this wine, thank you very much."

"Sure you do."

I raised my eyebrows at her. "Do you want a glass or not?"

Quinn stared at me and then let out a deep sigh. "I would. Thank you."

Something is weighing on her with that kind of sigh. I poured two glasses of the wine, hers having more in it than mine. While it wasn't my favorite alcohol to drink, the Moscato wasn't half-bad. Definitely drinkable.

We headed into the living room and settled onto the couch, the popcorn bowl between us. "So, you wanted to talk?"

She took a sip of her wine. "I do. About Chelsea."

I sat up a little straighter. "Did something happen? Is she okay?"

"Chelsea's fine. Nothing happened... yet."

"Yet? I don't like the sound of that."

Quinn shook her head, her eyes staring forward, not really focused on anything. "Me neither."

I shifted on the couch, flicking a quick glance over at my phone. *Why hasn't she texted or called yet?* When Quinn hadn't said anything for a minute, I prodded, "Are you bringing this up to me because you're a concerned friend who just needs to vent, or is there something you'd like me to do? You wouldn't be this on edge over nothing."

The woman sitting next to me played with the edge of her glass nervously. "If I tell you, Lukas can't know. Well, not right away... and not from you."

Oh damn. "You want us to hide this from him?"

Guilt and frustration flickered across her face. "I mean... well... yes, but no. I plan on telling him everything after you get more information. I don't want to blow this off, but I don't want to blow it out of proportion, either."

This wasn't typical Quinn. Hell, this wasn't how we took care of things in general. This was, however, a woman who had seen and lived through a lot of scary shit in the past few months, and I was more than willing to do a favor for her.

I nodded. "Okay. I'm going to need a few more details before I dive in. You know she's—"

"Important to you. Yeah, I know." She cut me off and then sighed. "She's important to me, too."

I nodded. Quinn settled in and dove into the story.

Rage flooded my bloodstream, and by the end, I understood

Lukas's reaction whenever Quinn was messed with. I wanted to pin Sylas to the wall and *educate* him on the proper and improper ways to treat women. No, I wanted to make him so he could never threaten anyone else ever again. *Keep it together until you get more information on the prick.* "I get why Chelsea doesn't want Lukas knowing. He'd do exactly what she's thinking he will. I have to at least tell Ryan so he can look into this guy, but unless this escalates into something bigger than I can handle on my own, I happily agree to keep this quiet." *Why didn't Chelsea tell me herself?*

Quinn nodded. "Thank you. That's all either of us are asking."

Looking far more calm than she had when first coming downstairs, she relaxed into the couch and grabbed the TV remote. "Want to watch more of that British baking show? It would be nice to watch it with someone who doesn't fall asleep while it's on."

I laughed a little. Lukas had lamented once or twice about getting in trouble for falling asleep while watching it. He had also thanked me at least a half-dozen times for watching it with her when he was gone. "Of course I do. It's bread week. You know it's going to be a good episode."

She grinned and queued up the recorded episode. Maybe it was working in close proximity to a fantastic baker, and maybe it was because it was a low-stakes, low drama show, but I was secretly obsessed with it and loved that Quinn asked me to watch it with her.

The hardest part of the entire hour was not taking my phone out of my pocket and texting Chelsea. Quinn and I had a strict no phone policy while watching our show, unless it was Lukas.

After the episode wrapped up, Quinn went back upstairs, and I waited a few minutes before checking all the cameras. Nothing out of the ordinary was there. After that, I headed up the stairs that led to the garage and did a quick walk around the house, making sure everything was secure from the outside.

After confirming the doors were all firmly shut and locked, and nothing was amiss on the property, I headed back downstairs and sat on the couch again. I had every intention of watching a movie, but as I stared at the dark TV, my thoughts drifted back to Chelsea. Like Quinn, she was a woman who never asked for anything unless it was absolutely necessary.

I was livid that some asshole was not only harassing her, but also threatening her. No one messed with me once I stepped in. A few had tried, but they quickly learned the error of their ways.

I wanted to be the guy to do something about this. I wanted to be the guy to make sure Chelsea was left alone to do what she pleased. I also wanted to be the guy she wanted to do things *with*. In the past few weeks, it was becoming harder to keep things professional. Once we kissed and then the whole Justin thing happened, all bets were off. She was always on my mind, and I wanted to spend all my time with her.

As I finished off the bottle of wine, I couldn't and didn't want to stay silent anymore. Grabbing my phone, I sent a text to Chelsea.

Phil: < Hey, you okay? >
Chelsea: < Yeah? Should I not be? >
I let out a deep breath.
Phil: < Why didn't you tell me about last night? >
Chelsea: < I see Quinn chatted with you. >

Not liking how this conversation was going, I needed to hear her voice and called her.

"You didn't want to text anymore?

"You know I'm here for you. However you need me."

There was a deep sigh on the other end of the call. "I know."

I stretched out on the couch and settled in for a long conversation. "Why didn't you tell me, Chels?"

"I thought I was fine."

The quiet hesitation of her voice rattled me. "Until?"

She was quiet for a moment. "Until I got to work and didn't see you right away. I didn't realize how important and calming it was for me to see you first thing in the morning."

"I didn't know it was that important, but now that I do, I'll make sure to be at the entrance in the morning."

"You don't have to."

I took a deep breath and let it out slowly. "What if I want to, Chelsea? What if I also feel better seeing you every morning? What if my heart is calmer after I've hugged you? What if smelling whatever perfume you wear is a balm to my jaded soul?" I knew I was putting it all out there, but I didn't care. We'd moved well past being *just* friends.

"Well... I... I feel better after hugging you, too. Hell, knowing you are in the building makes me feel better."

A ridiculously big smile spread across my face. "Well, it's settled then. We hug every morning, and you tell me when assholes are harassing and threatening you."

Chelsea chuckled. "I can live with that deal." She let out another deep sigh. "I'm sorry I didn't tell you last night ... or today. I think I was just more pissed and frustrated about the whole thing. I guess I didn't want to bother you with it."

"Chels... You're never a bother. I promise." *How do I make her see this? Accept this?* "Let me put this out there. I'd be happy to come out the next time you go out. I can lurk in the shadows or I can sit right there next to you. Your choice." A chuckle came out. "I mean, I know what I'd like to do, but this is your life, and I don't want to force your hand."

There was silence for a moment, long enough that I checked to see if the call dropped. *How do I balance work, protection, and play with her, especially when she's super independent and we sort of work together?* I got off the couch and wandered to my bedroom, where I promptly laid on my bed and stared at the ceiling. I knew with some careful consideration I'd be able to figure it out. Well, if Chelsea was open to it.

"I'd love for you to be there, but I also don't want to have to make sure I have a bodyguard sitting in the corner just to make sure I don't get harassed. I need to figure out a way for me to keep him away."

She was right. I flopped onto my bed and huffed out a breath. "I'm trying so hard not to jump in and take care of this for you. I know you can handle this. Hell, you can more than handle this..." I trailed off

"I know. And really, I appreciate everything. So much. You have no idea."

We wrapped up the call and I let out a deep sigh as I set the phone down on my chest. I was way more than just interested in Chelsea. *One thing at a time.*

Chelsea

The next morning I couldn't stop the cheesy grin that appeared on my face when I saw Phil standing next to my parking spot. By the time my car was parked and off, he was next to my door, waiting for me to open it.

I laughed as I stepped out of the car. "You could ha—"

Phil cut off my words as he pulled me into a tight hug and

kissed the top of my head. "Like I told you last night, I feel better after hugging you. And after the conversations I had with you and Quinn last night, I really needed to feel better."

I leaned into his embrace, letting out a deep breath. "Thank you." I loved how he never made me feel dumb or less than, no matter what I said.

When I started to pull away, he stopped me. "Nope. Not done yet."

A smile appeared on my face, and I glanced up. "I'm beginning to think you were worried about me."

His face snapped toward me as his eyes locked onto mine. The stare was intense, and it froze me where I stood. "Never doubt that I care about you and your happiness and safety."

I shook my head as I started into his dark brown eyes. "I never do." We stood there, staring at each other as if in a trance, until the slam of a car door startled me. "We should probably get inside."

Phil smirked, gave me one last squeeze, and stepped back. "Probably."

Chapter Fifteen

Chelsea

The rest of the week, almost every morning and every evening, Phil walked me to and from the lodge. If Phil wasn't there, for whatever reason, Quinn or Peter would walk me out. I nearly skipped out of the building with Quinn at the end of the day on Friday.

"Excited to see June tonight?"

I nodded. "She got called into work and will have to be behind the bar for a couple hours, but it will still be fun. I'm going to make sure of it."

"Good. Don't play hero, and don't let some dumbass ruin your night." Quinn gave me a quick hug before she and Phil headed off to her car. He winked at me, and I gave him a wave, hoping I wasn't turning bright red. *Should I have invited him? I know I wanted a fun girls night, but having him around would be fun, too.*

My drive home was uneventful, and I tossed my purse on the couch as I walked in the front door. As much as I wanted to change into a super sexy outfit for my night out, I didn't want to deal with any attention it could gather. I ran upstairs and pulled open my closet doors, staring at the wide variety in there. *There has to be something I can wear that's cute, comfy, and still bar appropriate.*

Minutes later, I was dressed in high-waisted skinny jeans, a royal blue fitted flannel shirt tied up at the waist with the sleeves rolled up, and my favorite blue high heels. I pulled my hair into a high ponytail, reapplied my favorite red, smudge-proof lipstick, and headed out, grabbing my purse and jacket along the way.

The three block walk to the bar was chilly, but not terrible considering it was in the middle of winter. When I walked in, the bouncer gave me a warm smile. "Good evening, Miss Chelsea."

"Hey, Dennis. Having a good night?"

The older gentleman nodded. "So far, so good."

"That's what I like to hear." I shrugged out of my burgundy down-filled coat and settled in on a stool at the end of the bar.

June walked over and let out a low whistle. "Damn. Someone's looking extra fine tonight."

I rolled my eyes. "It's just a flannel and jeans."

"Uh huh. Both of which hug all your curves and show off your assets. Don't play coy with me, Chels. You may not have gone all out in dressing up, but it doesn't mean you don't look hot." My best friend shook her head. "Anyway, you want your usual starter?"

I shook my head. "No. I'll go with whiskey on the rocks for now."

She tipped her head to the side and then nodded. "On it."

My drink was just about done when a martini glass with a light green liquid appeared in front of me. I looked up at my best friend. "What's this?"

She rolled her eyes. "Sour apple martini. It's from the idiot from the other night."

"Are you kidding me? Seriously? *He's* here tonight?" I wanted to look down the bar and see if Sylas was actually there, but I didn't want to acknowledge his presence or offer any means of encouragement. I also knew June wouldn't make up that kind lie.

"I wish I was. You don't have to drink it. Would you like me to bring another vodka cranberry?"

I snickered and finished off my drink, gently pushing away the martini glass. "I don't plan on it, and yes, please."

June quickly made and brought me a new drink before rushing off to cater to the sudden influx of patrons.

"You didn't like my gift?"

My hand clenched around the clear glass in my hand at hearing Sylas's grating voice. *Ignore him. He's not worth your time.* I took a deep breath and sipped *my* drink.

"Aw, come on Chelsea. Don't be like this."

I maintained my forward stare. "Don't be like *what* exactly, Sylas?"

He leaned against the bar, facing me. "Why the cold shoulder, babe?"

My grip tightened on my class as I slowly breathed in and out and counted to five. "I'm *not* your babe."

"I think we got off on the wrong foot last time."

Are you kidding me? No longer able to pretend he wasn't there, I turned toward the annoying idiot of a man. "Whatever gave you that idea?"

He shrugged and gave me a smile I knew he thought was charming, but it came off as smarmy. "Is it your time of the month? Were your crazy hormones taking over your ability to make good decisions? Any smart, calm, rational woman wouldn't lash out like that."

There's no way he just said that. I had to have misheard him. I stared at him, blinking several times. "Excuse me, the fuck, *what*?"

He gave me a look of pity. "Are the cramps still too much for you? I know how pain can mess with your mind. I thought the drink would have helped that. It's part of the reason I bought it for you. I wanted to help you relax and feel better. You seemed uptight the other night."

Glancing up at my best friend, I was met with the same stunned look that matched how I was feeling. "Is this really happening? Is he really standing next to me, spouting this bull-shit?" She gave me a nod, then glanced over my shoulder and smirked.

What's that about?

As I turned to look, Sylas moved and blocked my attempt. "I'm right here. You don't need to look anywhere else other than at me. You know as well as I do that I'm the best you're going to get here, even *with* your track record of attacking men."

He now had my complete and undivided attention. "What's that supposed to mean?"

Sylas took a step closer and leaned in. "It means I'm willing to give you a second chance at this, and remind you what happens if you cross my family."

"Are you threatening me *again*?" For as much rage that had been coursing through my body, it was quickly being replaced by ice cold fear.

"No. I'm giving you a chance to make things right."

I tensed up and was about to launch at him, but when I inhaled, the calming scent of Phil's cologne flooded my senses and gave me pause. *Is he here? Is that who June was smiling at?*

"There's that smile I knew you had for me. Like I said before, everyone likes me. You just needed to realize it."

"That smile wasn't for you." The words came out as a growl.

"Of course it was, sweetheart. You wouldn't break my heart by smiling at anyone else like that. You know I'm the guy for you." Sylas glanced around. "How about we go somewhere quieter so we can get cozy and have a little more fun."

He leaned forward and reached for my hand. I was about to panic when Phil appeared out of nowhere, wrapped his arm around my waist and kissed the top of my head.

"Chels, I'm so sorry I'm late. I had a client who called right as I was trying to leave, and it took a minute."

I'd never been so glad to see that man or be wrapped in his arms in my entire life. Sliding my hand up his arm, I gripped his sleeve tight. "Hey, sweetie. No problem. I get things happen sometimes." If my pet name surprised him, he didn't show it.

He shifted slightly, putting himself between me and Sylas, pulled me into a tighter hug, and leaned in so his lips were just touching my ear. "You seemed to be handling it just fine, but I'm here for backup if you need or want it."

I gave him an extra squeeze, trying to ignore how warm and tingly I felt being in his arms. "I appreciate that so much. He's worse than last time."

Phil took a step back and tucked a loose strand of hair behind my ear. Keeping an arm around me, he shifted to face Sylas. "I'm sorry. I completely interrupted you two. Where are my manners?" He held out his hand. "Hi. I'm Phil, Chelsea's boyfriend."

It took everything not to drop my jaw in shock or squeal like a pre-teen at her favorite band's concert. There had been no labels, but we definitely had been moving in that direction.

Phil

I have no idea why I said I was her boyfriend, but the stunned expression on the insufferable man's face was worth it. Chelsea's gasp of surprise both excited and worried me. *I'll deal with that fall out later.*

"Boyfriend? Since when? She never mentioned a boyfriend."

I wanted to punch this poor excuse of a man. "She doesn't owe you any personal information. All you need to know is that she's in good hands and you're welcome to leave."

His eyes narrowed at me. "I'm not going anywhere. It's a free country. I can sit here and have a drink if I want to."

"That works, too." I glanced down at Chelsea. "I know I promised you a fun night out, but the ambiance here has taken a nosedive. Want to take this home?"

She tipped her head back to look up at me. "Uh... Yeah. That sounds amazing, actually."

I waved over the bartender, who I noticed who was watching us with open interest. *Oh thank goodness, it's June.* "Is her tab settled?"

"Yep. She's all good."

I slid a twenty dollar bill across the bar. "I appreciate you looking out for her. Have a good night." I slide my hand from Chelsea's shoulder to her side, keeping her close to me. "Ready, hun?" She gave me a quick nod, her attention bouncing between me and Sylas as she slid her coat on.

I held her close to my side until we made it to the passenger side of my car where I turned her to face me. "Are you okay?"

She nodded. "Yeah. Thanks for the assist. He was starting to freak me out."

"He didn't hurt you, did he?"

Chelsea shook her head. "Nope. Barely laid a finger on me, thanks to you."

I let out a relieved breath and pulled her in for another hug. "Good." I held her longer than I should have, but now that she was in my arms, I didn't want to let her go. Ever. It was like a missing piece of me clicked into place, and my soul felt more whole. *Geez. Dramatic much?*

"So, boyfriend, huh?"

Her words pulled me from the dream-like state I never wanted to leave. I leaned back just enough to see her face. Before

I could respond, an angry, possessive voice sounded from behind us.

"Chelsea, there's no way you two are dating. He's so far out of your league. Like he'd want anything to do with you. I bet you had to pay him to hang out with you. I'm the only man who actually wants anything to do with you."

Seriously? This bullshit? Don't get into a fist fight with this loser. It's not worth the paperwork or getting yelled at by Lukas... or Quinn. Or would they even be upset because I protected her?

I turned to face Sylas, making sure I kept myself between him and Chelsea. "She doesn't want you. Leave."

He glared at me. "What are you going to do about it, pretty boy? Smile at me?"

Fuck it. Walking forward, I grabbed the front of his shirt and shoved him back until I had him pinned to the wall. "Listen here, asshole. First, she's out of both of our leagues. Second, I'm honored every day she wants to keep me in her life. Lastly, whether we are together or not, you have no chance with her. She's made that more than clear."

"You think your words mean shit to me? You're just some nobody here for a short time. Once you go back to whatever shit town you came from, Chelsea will be free for me to take and do with as I please."

I pulled my fist back and slammed it into his face, satisfied by the crunch that came from his nose. "You keep your fucking hands off her." With a shove that bounced his head off the brick wall, I turned and walked back toward Chelsea.

"Holy shit! Are you okay?"

I had every intention of grabbing Chelsea's hand and putting her in my truck to get her out of here, but I needed to remove the panic from her face. We had only ever been close in private and stolen moments, but I was tired of hiding, tired of the secrecy. After the conversation we'd had on the phone the other night, I wanted to back up my words. Taking her face in my hands, I pulled it to mine and kissed her.

Her lips felt even more amazing on mine tonight. The kiss started out gentle, but Chelsea quickly deepened it, making it possessive and everything I wanted and needed it to be.

My brain and rational thought finally kicked in. *We are standing in the middle of a parking lot.* I went to pull back, but Chelsea tightened her hold on me. "Oh, no. You stay right here. I'm not done with you just yet. Please don't overthink this and stop."

I smiled against her perfectly soft, plump lips and gave her another quick kiss. "Oh, I'm not going anywhere."

"Thank God. You have no idea how much I've been craving this." She ran her hands up my back, looping her arms around my shoulders and held me close as she kissed the hell out of me.

"Fine. I get it. You're fucking him. You didn't have to fuck him in the parking lot to prove your point."

I turned my head to the side, tightening my grip on the back of her coat as I tried not to be distracted by the kisses being trailed along my jaw. *She's good. Too good.* "No one's making you watch. Do you need help finding your car?"

The amorous exchange between me and Chelsea had excited more than just my mind, and I tried to pull away again, but she dropped her hands to my belt and pulled me against her. A knowing smirk was on her face when I returned my attention to her. "Is that your gun or are you happy to see me?"

"Honestly? Both." I winked.

Chelsea moved her hands from my belt and sank her fingers into my hair. "Glad to know it's not one-sided. I need more of you. Now." Then she pulled my face toward hers and pressed her lips to mine.

When her tongue teased my lips, and she tightened her grip on my hair, any remaining restraint I had left dissolved, and I leaned into the kiss, pressing her into the side of my truck. She was a siren, enticing me and heating my blood with every kiss, moan, and touch.

I had just enough presence of mind to clock when Sylas stormed off, muttering angrily under his breath. He slammed his car door and peeled out of the parking lot, squealing his tires on the way out.

Good.

I wrapped my arms around her waist and pulled Chelsea closer to me, returning her earlier teasing by trailing kisses along her jaw, nipping at the spot just behind her ears. She started to sink as her knees went out, but I held onto her tighter and leaned into my truck a little more.

My lips were on hers again, and I only stopped savoring her lips when my lungs demanded oxygen. I broke off the kiss and rested my forehead against hers, taking a deep breath. "He left a while ago, you know."

"Yeah, and?"

I let out a tiny chuckle. "I figured that show wasn't for him."

Chelsea stared into my eyes, lust and passion burning brightly. "What show?"

My heart tripped over itself as I reminded myself how to breathe. We were really doing this. We had been dancing around each other, flirting and sneaking kisses, but something in the way she was staring up at me let me know we were about to take things to another level. Every part of me was on board with that.

She tipped her head to the side and smiled as she released my hair and ran her fingertips along the short scruff on my jaw. "I wasn't kidding when I said I'd been dreaming about this."

A wide grin filled my face as I stared at her, stuck under the spell she'd cast on me. "What else did you dream about?"

Lust and excitement twinkled in her eyes. "A few more things, but I chalked them up to being crazy."

I leaned forward, lowering my head so my lips just touched her ear. "I'd love to hear more about your dreams, and I'd be honored to make them come true... if you're interested."

"How about we at least start with getting out of this parking lot?"

Staring at her lips, I asked, "My place or yours?"

She kissed the side of my neck, just below my ear. "Mine. It's closer."

"Perfect."

When I didn't immediately move, Chelsea ran her hands down the sides of my arms, resting them on my forearms. "You have to unpin me from the side of your truck first, Phil."

I kissed her forehead and stood up, straightening out some of her hair that had been tussled a bit in the moment of passion. "There you go again being as smart as you are beautiful."

Chelsea

After unpinning me from the side of his car, Phil opened the passenger door and waited for me to get situated in my seat before shutting it. *Holy shit. He punched Sylas in the face.* I glanced behind me, noticing Phil standing at the back of the truck on his phone. *Who is he talking to?* I didn't have long to wonder as he suddenly shoved the phone in his pocket, opened the door, and slid in.

"Ready?"

I reached out and took his hand in mine. "More than ready."

There was a low sizzle in the air between us during the short drive to my house that only intensified when he pulled into the driveway. The spark I felt when our skin touched as he helped me out of the truck had me swallowing hard in an attempt to keep control of myself. *Is this really, finally happening? If this is a dream, do not wake me.*

I pulled him close to me and wrapped my free arm around his neck, pressing a searing kiss into his lips. We stumbled our way to my front door, giggling, and stealing kisses along the way. You would have thought we were teenagers or drunk the way we were carrying on, but I didn't care. It felt like we were finally done sneaking around, and I was going to enjoy every moment of this.

When we made it to the door, he turned me, pressed me against it, and took my breath away with another of his mind-scrambling kisses. When he pulled away, I let out a shaky breath as I fumbled with my keys.

"You okay?"

I let out a breathy chuckle. "I'm so much more than okay."

Once I finally got the door open, I pulled him inside and pushed him against the wall next to the door, returning the favor by kissing the hell out of him. Phil somehow managed to close and lock the door without breaking the kiss.

It wasn't long before he was yanking my jacket off, and then his own, dropping both to the floor.

He spun us around, pinning me against the wall. "Where's your room, or do you want to stay down here?"

"I'm too old for the floor and it's way too drafty down here."

Phil snickered as he pushed my hair to the side and kissed my shoulder. "I know a way or two to keep you warm."

I'm sure you do. "Regardless, my bed is more comfortable and has the softest blankets to snuggle under later."

"Done."

He scooped me up, carried me upstairs, and after some direction from me, found my room and tossed me on the bed. I had barely stopped bouncing before he had moved over to my dresser and began to unarm himself. Seeing him place his weapon and holster on top didn't cool the flame burning inside me. If anything, the reminder he was gorgeous, armed, *and* dangerous was a huge turn on that had me wanting him even more. He was being smart and careful, but I couldn't stop myself from making a joke. "Good idea. Wouldn't want you to accidentally shoot your shot early."

Phil snorted and shook his head as he turned and headed for me. "Don't worry. When I shoot anything, it won't be accidental, and it most certainly *won't* be early."

We'll see about that soon enough. "Promises, promises."

He let out a low chuckle while crawling up the bed toward me. "Oh, I'll be making good on that promise, and more than once if I have anything to say about it." He slowly unbuttoned my shirt, trailing kisses down the freshly exposed skin. I let out a moan when he finally pushed the flannel off my shoulders, unhooked my bra, and worshiped me with his mouth. His lips on my skin felt like licks of flame as he made his way down my neck and over the curve of my breast, making sure to take his precious time. Pleasure sizzled in my blood as his hands caressed my sides and my hips, lovingly following my curves as if he was memorizing every inch.

Phil unbuttoned my jeans and slowly slid them down, continuing the slow, sensual assault down my body. The things he was doing with his tongue were mind-blowing. I don't know why it surprised me, especially with how well he kissed.

The only reason I knew my pants had completely come off was because he was in-between my legs and his hands were slowly massaging their way up. The groan that came out of my mouth wasn't just from carnal pleasure, the man knew how to massage. *If this is just foreplay, am I ready for the rest?*

His fingers found their way to my center, as did his mouth. The swirling and kissing he was doing had me rolling my hips, and it did not take him long to have me writhing in ecstasy and shouting his name as stars burst behind my closed lids and pleasure coursed through my system.

Holy shit. That was amazing.

A soft chuckle filled my ears as I caught my breath. "You still with me?"

I turned my head to the side and opened my eyes just enough to see Phil stretched out next to me. The smug grin on his face would have normally irritated me, but he'd earned it. I was still gathering my scattered wits from the mind-blowing orgasm he'd just delivered. "Glad to know you're more than just a pretty face. Damn. Give me a sec, and I'll show you *just* how much I appreciated that."

Wrapping his free arm around me, he pulled me close and kissed me. "That's not all I'm good at."

We made out for a bit while caressing and rubbing against each other, before I shifted and went to crawl on top of him.

He grabbed my hips, stopping me from mounting him like I wanted to. "Condom?"

Right. Do I have one? "Um... yes... but..."

"Don't worry. I got this." Phil reached over and grabbed one off my bedside table.

How did that get there? I couldn't help but shake my head a little as I took the foil packet from his hands and ripped it open. "Were you planning for this all along?"

He shook his head, lust still heavy in his eyes. "Nope. That doesn't mean I can't be prepared, though."

"I suppose not." I rolled the condom along his length, impressed and quite pleased with what was in my hands. "Ready?" I winked at him.

His grip tightened on my hips again, pulling my core closer to what we both craved. "Bring me to my knees."

The power and confidence he had in me was overwhelming and intoxicating. He was literally giving the control to me. I must have locked up, because the next thing I knew he was sitting up and my face was in his hands.

"Are you sure you're good with this? We can wait."

The concern and care in his eyes nearly undid me, and I shifted, sliding him into me. "Oh, I definitely want this. I've just never had a guy hand over all the control. Not that I mind. It just caught me off guard."

Phil rolled his hips as he pulled me in for a searing kiss, short-circuiting my brain and reminding me of exactly what I was working with.

I shoved him back, flat on his back again, slowly sliding down his length. A sigh came out, and I couldn't help but notice how his eyes glazed over and his mouth dropped open at the feel of me sheathing him. *Glad I'm not the only one impressed.* Leaning back for a better angle, I rocked my hips slowly, savoring the amazing sensation of how full I felt. I took my time, thoroughly enjoying everything Phil had to offer when he started thrusting harder and his fingers started rubbing a certain over-sensitized nub. "Oh my God, yes." I picked up the pace, and so did he, slamming into me as I met his thrusts. Not too much later, that delicious pleasure was building inside me again. When I looked down at Phil, his jaw was clenched and the veins were sticking out in his neck with the effort he was exerting to hold off for me.

Pressing his lips to mine, he panted, "Give it to me, Chels."

His raw voice shot through me, bringing me over that edge and igniting my climax, and he joined me a few thrusts later. Once it finally began to ease, I collapsed forward, laying on his chest.

He rubbed my back as I caught my breath for the second time that night. "Damn."

"Hmm?" My head was still on him, coming down from my euphoric high.

"You might have just ruined me." His ab muscles tensed as he half sat up to kiss the top of my head. "You're fucking amazing."

We laid there, wrapped in each other's arms until I shivered from the chill in the air and was reminded how full my bladder was. I picked up my head. "As much as I don't want to move, I need to pee and find some clothes before I fall asleep."

Phil pouted when I sat up, and ran his hand down my arm. "You don't need to put on anything for my benefit. I'll keep you plenty warm."

I leaned over and kissed him. "It's too cold to go commando. I don't care how hot you are."

He chuckled as I stood up and headed toward the bathroom. "Fair enough. I need to take care of a couple things before passing out myself, but ladies first."

After taking care of what I needed to in the bathroom, I wrapped myself in a towel and sauntered out.

Phil kissed me on the head as I walked past him and then headed in the bathroom himself. "Save a spot in the bed for me."

"I hope you're good with being the little spoon, because I am the ultimate cuddler." I shot him a grin as he shook his head and closed the door.

Chapter Sixteen

Phil

Sex with Chelsea was amazing and surpassed every expectation. Sleeping cuddled up next to Chelsea was equally as fantastic. It took a second to get used to being the little spoon, but when I shifted to laying on my back, she kept herself wrapped around me like a koala bear. I'd never slept better.

I vaguely heard an alarm going off, but then it stopped. She snuggled into my side, and I drifted off again.

The next thing I knew I was cold and being shaken, and when I opened my eyes to see what was going on, Chelsea was leaning over me. "Finally. Good morning, sleepy head."

"Good morning." I smirked and rolled onto my side, pulling Chelsea closer to me. "Hm? What's going on?"

"Some spectacular bodyguard you are. Both of our alarms have gone off, and I've been trying to wake you up for ten minutes."

"What time is it?"

"6:52am"

"What?" I sat up with a start, launched myself out of bed, and scrambled to collect my clothes and get dressed. "Shit. I thought I heard it go off. I need to get back to the house so I can take Quinn to work."

Chelsea sat in the middle of the bed, failing at keeping her amusement contained. "Nice shirt."

I glanced down and burst out laughing at the fact I was trying to slide on her flannel shirt. "Well that explains why I couldn't get it past my elbow." I tossed the shirt at her, picked up my black t-shirt, and pulled it on.

"Promise to talk more later?"

I bent down and kissed her, letting my lips linger there a moment longer than I should have, before pulling away and smiling. The lust in her eyes was almost enough to make me call Peter and ask him to take Quinn. *You can see her later. Be responsible and go to work.* "Promise to do a lot more than just talk later."

"I'd like more of this, in any variation, happening again. This was not just a one-night thing for me."

Coming to lean in front of her, and staring into those blue eyes, I kissed her quickly, and pressed my forehead against hers. "Same for me, Chels. *So* not a one-night thing." I kissed her one more time, growling at the restraint it took not to stay, and headed out to my car before I could change my mind. Once settled into the driver's seat, I started the engine and raced back to the house.

Seeing all the cars in the garage filled me with relief. Everyone was still here. I rushed toward the hidden entrance to the basement and hurried down the stairs. *I can do this. I can still be on time.*

Peter looked up from the bowl of cereal he was eating and raised an eyebrow when I burst into our basement apartment. "Are you just *now* getting in? Where were you?"

I rushed past him toward the bathroom. "Harass me later. I need to be upstairs in less than fifteen minutes."

"You know I can take Quinn to work, right?"

"And have to explain to her *why?* No thanks."

I took the fastest shower of my life and dressed in all black. I knew it would match, and time was of the essence.

Quinn shot me a curious glance when I walked into the kitchen, smoothing my hair back. "Did I hear the garage door open and close a few minutes ago?"

"Um... yeah. That was me."

She raised an eyebrow. "Everything okay?"

Act normal. "Yep. Everything's great."

She studied my face a little longer, as if she was searching for something, and then a knowing grin spread across her face. "Did you just get in from making sure Chelsea was okay?"

I stopped in the middle of the room. "Um... maybe?"

"Are you good to take me to work?"

"Of course. That's why I'm up here."

Quinn shook her head, trying not to laugh as she stood up and shrugged into her jacket. "Well, I'm ready to head out when you are."

The car ride was quiet until I pulled into our usual parking spot and turned off the engine.

"Hold on a sec before you get out."

Here it comes. I glanced up to look in the rear-view mirror. "Everything okay?"

Quinn's attention was squarely focused on me. "Can I be frank with you?"

Panic coursed through me at her tone and demeanor, not that I let it show on my face. It overwhelmed the need to snicker and make a joke about acting like her boss. "Of course. What's up?"

"Chelsea is one of my dearest friends out here. I know you have a thing for her, and I know you were helping her out with the guy problem, but I swear to all that's good and holy, if you hurt her, I will use you for target practice, and Lukas will only get to deal with what's left over. Got it?"

I held Quinn's gaze in the mirror. "I have no intention of hurting her."

She arched her left eyebrow in the most slow and terrifying way. "Intentional or not, I meant what I said. You will not hurt my girl. Understood?"

"Yes, ma'am." I had no doubt Quinn would make my death look like an accident if I crossed her.

She stared at me a moment longer before nodding. "Good. Now that we've settled *that*, shall we head in?"

I nodded and hurried out of the car so I could open Quinn's door. She laid her hand on my forearm and gave it a squeeze. "I know you'll do right by her. I just needed to say my two cents."

"Thank you, and I respect that."

We walked into the building, and I watched as she headed to her office. Once her door was closed, I made my way toward the security office, giving Chelsea a smile and a wink as I passed the front desk.

As soon as I was in the office, I dropped into one of the rolling chairs, sank my head into my hands, and let out a long, slow breath.

"That bad of a morning?"

I glanced up at Borce, the head of security at the lodge, and shook my head. "No. I just got a reminder of why it would be incredibly stupid to piss off Quinn."

The older man narrowed his eyes at me. "Do I want to know what you did?"

"Who said I did anything?"

He shook his head and rolled his eyes. "You're pale and slightly shaky. Also, you're not gloating with pride about her putting some poor, unfortunate soul in their place. The bread-crumb trail was pretty easy to follow."

I chuckled. "Fair enough. Well, I didn't do anything, but I got a warning shot *if* I did."

Borce let out a low chuckle as he turned back toward the wall of surveillance monitors. "That warning shot was a kindness, and you know it."

I knew it was, but it still didn't stop a smile from appearing on my face. Chelsea was worth all the heat.

Chelsea

Phil smiled at me as he headed off to wherever he needed to be. I gave a little wave back and tried to ignore how hot my face felt. *How am I supposed to work near him after last night?*

It was as if the gods were listening, I was too busy taking care of guests, answering the phone, and tidying up the Reading Room to overthink the potential fallout from our amazing night together.

I breathed out a small sigh of relief when the late morning calm hit. It gave me a chance to tidy up the front desk and finish up some paperwork. I checked my phone and was pleased to see a message from a familiar name.

Phil: < hope your day is fantastic. I'll try to swing by later. >

Phil: < By the way, Quinn knows. She heard me come in this morning. >

Chelsea: < It already had a fantastic start. I have high hopes for the rest of the day. >

Chelsea: < So what if she knows? It's not illegal for us to hang out and enjoy each other's company. >

Or other things. I couldn't help the grin that appeared on my face.

I'd barely slid my phone back into my pocket when a plate with a few cookies appeared in front of me.

"Have a minute?"

I glanced to my left and saw Quinn standing next to me, holding a mug of coffee.

"For you? Always." I piled up my papers and set them to the side, happily taking one of the cookies. A groan came out as I took a bite. "How do Edith's cookies always taste so amazing?"

"I have no idea, but I don't care." Quinn snickered as she took a cookie for herself and settled onto one of the stools we hid under the counter. "So, last night went really well, I take it?"

My face went hot and I almost choked on the piece of cookie I was chewing. "Um, yeah. You could say that."

"And Phil *connected* with you at the bar?"

Boy did he. I made myself busy sanitizing keys and keychains, not able to look Quinn in the eye. "Yep."

"Just so you know, you two aren't fooling anyone with this innocent 'nothing happened here' act you're both miserably failing at. He rolled into my house less than a half hour before I had to leave. I hardly think he was protecting you from Sylas all night."

I let out a deep breath. "Well, he appeared at my side, informing Sylas he was my boyfriend, then... something shifted. I can't quite pinpoint what caused it to happen, but we went from him 'rescuing' me and telling Sylas to go away... and the next thing I knew, we were making out against the side of his car."

Quinn snickered. "You really can't figure out how you ended up all over... or under... the man you've been pining over, and stealing private moments with for weeks?"

My face grew hot. She wasn't wrong. I knew exactly what happened to shift the act into reality. Phil had defended me without demeaning me, to the point of getting into a fight. It was hot, and I'd jumped at the opportunity to 'thank' him. "I mean... I'd had a couple drinks, so my inhibitions were lower..." My best friend gave me a heated look, and while I tried to keep the heat from my cheeks, and knew I failed miserably when she chuckled.

"Oh, shut up. He was telling Sylas that I was out of both of their leagues, punched him, and then he... he bent down and kissed the hell out of me. When he pulled back, I refused to let him go, and we kissed again. It sort of escalated from there."

Quinn's smirk widened. "Right. *Sort of.*"

I bit the inside of my lip. "Well... He took me home..."

"Where you continued to enjoy the evening. I figured out that much."

This was not the conversation I thought I'd be having at work, especially at the front desk. "Yeah... He slept through his alarm, I woke him up, and then he ran out of my house like there was a fire... well, after saying a sweet goodbye."

She shook her head and stood up. "Try not to get him into too much trouble." Quinn took a step to leave and then turned to face me. There was a mischievous twinkle in her eye. "I'll stop harassing you and leave you to your work. Have a good day." She left the lobby and headed back to her office.

A whole two minutes before Phil appeared. "Everything okay out here?"

I narrowed my eyes and shot him a playful glare. "Were you watching the cameras to make sure Quinn had cleared out before visiting me?"

He chuckled as the faintest hint of a blush tinted his cheeks. "Maybe."

"She's worried about you getting in trouble."

Phil let out a low breath. "Yeah, she gave me the warning shot earlier about what would happen if I hurt you in any way. I was a little worried she would be mad, but..."

I tipped my head to the side and reached out to grab his hand. "Were you *really* that worried?"

"A little. I've got a really sweet gig working here. Lukas and Frank are amazing bosses, and I'd hate to screw that up." He stepped closer to me and traced the top of my hand with his fingertip. "I'm afraid to screw up whatever this is, too."

My heart skipped a beat and raced all at the same time. "Yeah?"

He nodded. "Oh yeah."

"You still want more of what happened between us yesterday?"

"One hundred percent."

I held his gaze for a long moment before giving him a wide smile as red blossomed over his cheeks. "Then come over for dinner tonight."

"Yes, ma'am." He squeezed my fingers, and then headed back to the security office. Watching as he walked down the hall, I was not ashamed to admit how much I enjoyed the view.

Chapter Seventeen

A few months later.

Chelsea

I had barely hung up the phone and was getting ready to call Frank and take a break when Lukas and Ryan entered the lobby, walking with purpose. There wasn't enough urgency to make me think it was a full-on emergency, but it was still enough to put me on edge.

"Where's Quinn?"

"In her office, why?"

Lukas nodded at Ryan, who immediately headed in that direction.

"Lukas, what's going on? Is she in danger? Did something happen?"

He studied my face for a moment and then let out a sigh. "Maybe. Where's Frank?"

"In *his* office."

Lukas nodded again. "I'll be right back."

Oh, what the hell? I watched him make his way down that hallway and glanced around the lobby. It was empty. The Reading

Room was empty. Security had relaxed slightly in the past couple months, and while there was no longer a constant second shadow near the entrance, I knew they weren't far away.

Just about the time I was pulling my phone out to text Phil, Frank and Lukas walked into the lobby. "Chelsea, you're good to go for the day."

"What?" About the same time, Ryan and Quinn also joined us. I looked toward Quinn, noting the extremely tense look on her face. "What in the hell is going on?"

She rolled her eyes and shook her head. "We are apparently getting a day or two off."

Her answer didn't make me feel any better. I was enjoying the normal we'd all settled into. *Please let this be an overreaction.*

Lukas nodded at Frank. "Again, I'm sorry, and I promise I'll cover here as best as I can."

Hands landed on my shoulders. "I'll take her to her house to grab some things and then bring her over."

Phil's voice and presence washed over me and helped temper the worst of the fear and frustration.

Lukas stared at him for a moment. "Fine. Ryan will go with you. Be quick about it." He pulled Quinn into a tight hug, whispered something in her ear, kissed the side of her head, and escorted her from the building.

"Let's go." Phil slid his arm around my waist and guided me to the car waiting just outside.

He'd just gotten both of us into the car when my thoughts exploded. "Wha—"

My words were cut off with a hard, quick kiss. "I swear I'll explain everything once we're at the house, just please trust us right now."

"Okay." I nodded, stunned by the very quick turn of events. It was clearly important that he and the guys get Quinn and I out of there ASAP. The flurry of activity reminded me of the day Quinn and Lukas were taken, except this time I was the one being swept away to go to a safe place.

I wasn't sure what was more significant, the fact I trusted Phil and the guys implicitly and didn't want to argue, or that he kissed me so publicly. Even though we were together, and everyone knew it, we still tried to keep things professional at work, especially when we were both on duty.

"Thank you." Phil kissed the side of my head and wrapped his arm around me, pulling me close to him. We both knew I was more than capable of kicking ass, but I leaned into his side and let him protect me. I liked knowing I didn't have to do it on my own, and he seemed to relax ever so slightly when I didn't fight him.

Is this how it's always going to be? A constant, unknown roller-coaster of events that might have me pulled out of work and whisked away?

Phil kept his arm around me the entire drive to my house, but asked me to stay in the truck with Ryan while he checked to make sure everything was safe.

After a few minutes of silence, I couldn't take it anymore. "Am I in danger?"

The brunette man in the front seat glanced up into the rear view mirror before letting out a sigh and resuming his surveillance of our surroundings. "Yes and no. The situation is still developing, but we didn't want to take any chances waiting. We'd rather have you inconvenienced for a day or two than have something bad happen."

I had anticipated being brushed off, so his more than one word answer surprised me. "Oh. Well, thank you. I knew Quinn was the priority. I don't know when I was added to that list."

Ryan turned around to face me. "You're a priority to Phil, which makes you a priority to the rest of us. We protect our people, Chelsea. You know that."

I glanced toward the house, watching Phil walk through my front door. *Please be safe.*

Phil

I was on edge the second I slid her key into the door and opened it. The information Ryan had shared with the team only an hour ago wasn't complete, but Chelsea and her well-being was at the center of it, and it was enough to warrant putting her and Quinn in lockdown until we could confirm more details. *Fucking Sylas.*

As I walked up to her porch, I noticed the welcome mat was pushed aside and there were scratches in the paint on the front door. It hadn't looked like that two nights ago when I had been over. Something was off. Very off. *What else is going on?*

My question was immediately answered when I opened the door and stepped inside. Chelsea's place was trashed. Someone had been in there and had not only slashed the hell out of her couch, but the coffee table was flipped over, the recliner was on its side, and the painting that had been above the fireplace mantle was now on the floor.

My gun was out and in front of me as I quietly made my way through the living room.

"Chelsea, I've got your little boy toy up here. You might want to get up here and plead for his life."

Sylas? Desperate little prick. I glared at the stairs. While that may have worked for her, I wasn't going to fall for the trap, especially since I *was* that boy toy.

Phil: < Sylas is in here - might not be alone - room trashed on main floor. >

Ryan: < Purple is with me. Do you need backup? >

Phil: < If I'm not out in 5, yes. Heading up hot. >
Lukas: < Keep us informed. >

I slid the phone back in my pocket and sent a prayer up to anyone listening. *And this is why we removed Chelsea and Quinn from work.* It was dangerous to go into this blind, but I knew there was back up outside. Making my way up the stairs, I listened for anything that might tip me off as to what was waiting for me in her bedroom.

"Babe, don't feel like you have to sneak up the stairs. I know you're here. The longer you take, the less likely you'll be able to save his life. How much blood can someone lose and not die?"

Rage surged through me as I thought about what Chelsea's reaction would have been if she had walked in that door instead of me. She would have raced like hell upstairs to save me. If I didn't know *exactly* where Chelsea was, and that she was safe and protected with Ryan, I would be freaking the fuck out. *This fucker is so dead.* After taking a deep breath, I stepped into the doorway and aimed at his chest.

His eyes went wide as he reached for his gun. "You're not Chels—" The explosions from my gun covered the rest of his words, and a stunned expression appeared on his face. "You... Shot... Me."

Way to state the obvious. "I did. I know all about what you were planning to do to Chelsea, and I didn't appreciate it. Neither did she."

Sylas grabbed his chest where two crimson stains were growing larger, and into one large stain. "Where... where is she?"

I stared at him, my gun still trained on his chest. "Exactly where she *should* be."

He shook his head and grabbed the corner of Chelsea's dresser as he stumbled forward. "No. She... She's supposed to be here... Wait... What time..." He looked around wildly, trying to find the clock on her bedside table.

"Time for you to leave my girlfriend the fuck alone." I quickly glanced around the room, seeing if there was anything else noteworthy. My chest tightened when I saw the roll of duct tape and a syringe on the bed.

That's how they got Lukas and Quinn. That can hardly be a coincidence.

Sylas collapsed onto his knees. "You won't get away with this." The wet gurgle in his breathing was getting worse.

"Get away with what? Protecting someone I love? I'm pretty sure men get applauded for things like that. What they *don't* get away with," I crouched down so we were eye to eye, making sure I kept him in my sights, "Is threatening women. Not on my watch."

"Well aren't you a..." He gasped, "a fucking boy scout. Want an award?"

A dry chuckle came out. "No. I earned them all already."

"I don't care. . . you can't stop everything." Sylas groaned. "There's ... too much in motion. You may get this win, but... but they... they are still going to take you down..." He took a strained breath and a deranged grin spread across his face, "and win it all."

I hit him across the face with my gun, knocking him to the floor. "You don't get to tell me what I can and can't do." Before he had a second to respond, I hit him in the temple with the butt of my gun and knocked him to the ground, where he went still.

Checking my phone, I realized my five minutes were almost up.

Phil: < Neutralized the target - vitals fading - packing for purple - location will need deep clean. >

Lukas: < Noted. I need the three of you here first. >

I took several pictures, making sure to document the syringes, sent them to Ryan, and then went about searching for a suitcase. I found one in the bottom of her closet and tossed it on her bed. As I went to step over Sylas's form, I stopped and watched his chest. The blood stain was still growing, but his breaths were slow and shallow. *It shouldn't be long now.*

After watching him for another moment, I headed into the bathroom, wanting to grab as many of Chelsea's things as I could before leaving. I had no clue how long she'd have to stay out of her townhouse once we left. *At least she will be alive and safe.*

Fifteen minutes later I was confident I'd grabbed all the basics, and a few extra things as well. A smile crossed my lips when I opened and reached into the bottom of her pajama drawer, and I couldn't help but add some of the contents of it to the suitcase.

My phone buzzed in my pocket, and I knew I needed to wrap it up and get the hell out of here. I set her suitcase outside the room and turned around to check Sylas again. Feeling for the pulse on his neck, it took me a moment before I found it. It was slow and very weak. His fingertips were already turning purple, and I knew the man had only minutes to live, at best.

I checked my phone.

Lukas: < Vitals? >

Phil: < Weak and fading quickly. >

Lukas: < Clear out. >

As I made my way downstairs, I shook my head. Chelsea was going to be devastated when I told her about this. *I'll wait until we're in my apartment.*

Careful to make sure the door was locked, I closed it and headed outside. After securing Chelsea's luggage in the back, I slid into the backseat, pulling my girl close.

Locking eyes with Ryan in the rear-view mirror, I gave him a pointed look. "We need to go. *Now.*"

Ryan nodded and nearly peeled out of the driveway. We both were on high alert, and I could feel in the faint tremble of Chelsea's muscles that told me she was freaked out.

"Phil?"

I pulled her closer and kissed the top of her head. "Someone was waiting for you in your house when I walked in."

She sat up with a start. "What?"

I nodded. "That's what took me so long. I had to take pictures of the damage, make it so they weren't a problem, and then pack up some things for you. I think I grabbed everything you needed."

"*Damage?* And the person, did you kill them? Phil, what aren't you telling me?" Chelsea looked around. "Where are we going now?"

"The house."

"Lukas and Quinn's place?"

I nodded, letting out a deep sigh. "Looks like we are putting some of it to use sooner than expected."

Chelsea glanced at Ryan and then looked at me again. "Let me guess, this is also part of the later conversation?"

"Something like that, yeah."

She rested her head on my shoulder and tightened her grip on my arm. "You'd better, or I'm going to Lukas. I went head to head with his brother, and his dad smiled and introduced himself after. Trust me when I say Quinn isn't the only one who doesn't have any hesitation about getting in his face."

Ryan's eyebrows went up as he glanced up at me in the mirror. The look he gave me was a smirk that said, *You have your hands full with her.*

I nodded. *Don't I know it?*

It wasn't long before we were pulling into the driveway and directly into the middle stall of the three-car garage.

Ryan parked, turned off the car, and turned to face me. "Take

Chelsea downstairs through your entrance and stay there. I'll be down with an update as soon as I can."

I nodded and hopped out of the car, quickly retrieving her suitcase from the trunk. By the time I turned around again, she was standing next to me. I slid my hand into hers and led her toward the hidden basement entrance.

Her eyes went wide when I unlocked and opened what looked like a tall cabinet door to reveal a staircase. "What's this?"

I flipped on the light switch, and for the first time that day a small smile crossed my face. "My place."

Chelsea stared at me for a moment. "I know you live here. Why are you rifling through a cabinet right now?"

"Come on."

Nerves exploded in my stomach as we made our way down the stairs. It was one thing to bring someone home after a date, but it was an entirely different thing to bring home someone this important to protect them and keep them safe.

Chelsea

He has a secret entrance?

When Phil opened the door at the bottom of the stairs, the last thing I expected to see was a cozy looking living room. As I looked around the basement, I was stunned to see what looked like a normal apartment. "It doesn't look anything like a basement."

Phil chuckled as he set down my luggage. "Did you think Peter and I lived with cinder block walls and bare mattresses on the floor?"

"Well, no. I knew there was an apartment down here, I've just never seen this nice of a finished basement before."

"Fair enough. Would you like the rest of the tour?"

I turned to face him and grabbed the front of his shirt. "I want answers, Phil. What in the hell is going on? I've complied and played nice and kept my attitude in check, but I'd be lying if I said I wasn't completely freaking out."

He nodded. "You want to sit on the couch or a bed when we talk?"

A dry laugh came out. "I... a bed, I think." The adrenaline rush of it all was wearing off, and I wanted and needed to lie down for a second.

"Okay." Phil led me to a room, closing the door behind us after setting down my suitcase. Never letting go of my hand, he walked over to the queen-size bed centered on the wall and gently pulled me into his lap. Only then did he let out a deep sigh. "I'm so glad I was the one who went into your house today and not you."

"Are you going to tell me anything, or just be annoyingly vague and keep me in the dark?"

"Sylas was in your bedroom, waiting for you. And from the looks of it, he was going to do the same thing to you as Quinn and Lukas."

Holy shit. After the little showdown in the parking lot between Phil and Sylas, and when I never heard from or saw the man again, I thought he'd taken the hint and stayed away. An involuntary shudder ran down my spine, and Phil tightened his hug. After taking a deep breath, questions popped into my head. "Why did Lukas and Ryan come to the lodge in the first place?"

"Ryan intercepted a conversation between Sylas and an unknown person. Your name was specifically mentioned, and your workplace, and the location of your house. The original plan was to have you pack a bag to stay here a night or two while we got to the bottom of it, but now that your house has been severely compromised, you're here for a bit."

"Severely compromised?" I swallowed my fear down for a moment. "How bad is it?"

He stared at me for a long moment. "Do you really want to see it right now? We can wait. The pictures aren't going anywhere."

"I'd rather get all the bad news at once and then move forward from there."

A few moments passed before Phil shifted and pulled his phone out of his pocket. He tapped on the screen a few times and then handed it to me. "Here."

My stomach sank and I almost dropped the phone when I saw the destruction of my living room. "I loved that couch." Paralyzing fear shot through me, and I actually did drop the phone when I saw the duct tape and the loaded syringe. "Holy shit."

Phil caught the phone before it hit the ground.

Quinn: < Holy shit. Are you okay? Is Chelsea okay?! >

Seeing Quinn's text message pop down on the top of the screen helped slow down the looming anxiety attack.

He typed out a response and set the phone down before facing me. "What do you need from me right now? How can I make you feel better? Can I even do anything to help?"

I nodded. "Just hold me." When his arms tightened, something deep within me cracked, and tears came and rolled down my face. It was one thing for Sylas to be a threatening ass at the bar, but knowing he broke into my house, trashed the place, and then waited there to possibly drug and kidnap me? It was too much to process. Phil rubbed my back, kissed the side of my head, and whispered encouraging words while I clung to him and let my hysterics out.

Once I was able to take a deep breath without it coming out, I sagged into his arms.

"Better?"

"For now, yeah. Thank you."

There was a soft knock at the door. "Chelsea? Can I come in?" It was Quinn's voice.

Phil looked down at me. "You up for a Quinn chat?"

I nodded. I had a feeling she was freaking out, too.

"Come on in."

The door immediately burst open, and Quinn rushed into the room and knelt in front of me. "Holy shit, Chels. Are you okay?"

"I'm fine. I was in the car with Ryan the whole time. Never saw a thing."

Quinn looked up at Phil. "You're my favorite today."

He smirked. "Not Lukas?"

She shook her head. "While he did make sure we all stayed safe, he didn't deal with a crazed lunatic today. You did. Thank you."

"Just do—"

"Oh my god, cut the humble act and take the freaking compliment and gratitude, will you?"

Phil took a deep breath and let it out slowly. "You're welcome. I'm glad I was there."

"Thank you." Quinn stood up and then wrapped us both in a hug. "I'm glad you're both okay. Lukas didn't want me to come down and bother you, but like I'm going to let him tell me what I can and can't do in my own house."

I snickered. *That's my girl.*

"Well, now that I've seen you're both upright and okay, I can go start dinner for all of us without the looming anxiety. Promise me you'll let me know if either of you need anything before then."

"Will do."

She nodded and left.

We sat in silence for a moment before realization finally hit. *He put his life on the line... for me.* Shifting, I moved so I was straddling Phil's lap, wrapped my arms around his neck, and stared deep into his eyes. "You could have died today."

His hands slid onto my hips as he let out a soft chuckle and shook his head. "Not a chance, Chels. Not when I have so much to live for."

My breath froze in my throat. "What?"

He tightened his grip on my hips. "You know how important you are to me."

"Well, yeah..." I trailed off, not sure where my thoughts were going.

He reached up and tucked a loose hair behind my ear before holding my face in his hands. "You're one of the most important things in the world. I don't know if I'd be able to recover if something happened to you."

My heart hurt from how happy I was hearing those words. "Is that why you clung to me in the car like I was going to disappear?"

Phil chuckled and kissed me. "Yes."

My lips tingled from the brief kiss, and I wanted more. "I'm going to need more confirmation that you're okay."

"Oh?"

I nodded as I kissed his neck and started to unbutton his shirt. "Yes. I need to make sure every inch of you is perfect.

His eyes lit up, and his breath quickened as the other meaning of my words clicked. "I'm more than willing to do anything it takes to make you feel better."

"Then help me by taking off your pants."

A low chuckle came out. "Yes, ma'am."

By the time I had wiggled out of my skirt and underwear, Phil was pulling me back toward the bed. "I can take care of it from here. You're not the only one who needs to make sure the person they love is okay."

I had been in the middle of kissing his neck when the word hit me and I froze in place. *Love?* We'd been dating since our first night together after he saved me at the bar. Things had been getting more serious between us since then, but we hadn't used the 'L' word yet. For all the anxiety and panic that has been threatening to consume me, his use of that one small but mighty word had my heart wanting to explode from happiness.

"Chels?"

My head popped up and I locked my attention on his face. "You love me?"

Phil nodded, a goofy grin now all over his face. "A lot."

I pressed my lips to his and kissed him with everything I had. My hands were in his hair, clinging to him, and when I finally broke the kiss, I rested my forehead against his. "I'm so glad, because I love you, too."

His face lit up like a Christmas tree. "Yeah?"

I rocked my hips, grinning when I slid back a little and felt him hard. "A lot." I shifted and slid onto him, grinning at how his eyes immediately glazed over with lust.

"I need to see all of you."

I sat up, groaning in delight with how full I felt at this angle, and was more than happy to let the man I loved, and who loved me back, relieve me of the rest of my clothing.

We were just settling into a rhythm that had my pleasure building when Phil's phone started ringing.

Phil grumbled as he looked over at it. "This had better be fucking important."

I was determined not to lose the momentum we had going and kept rolling my hips against his. "Do you have to answer it?"

He pulled me tight to his chest, giving me a quick kiss. "It's Lukas... It's his ringtone. He'll come down here if I don't. Do you want that?"

Lukas would be in for one hell of a surprise if he did. I let out a frustrated sigh. "No." As Phil reached over for the phone, I tightened certain core muscles and pulled a groan from Phil.

"Chels, You can't do that when I'm on the phone."

A wicked grin crossed my face. "Answer the call and make it quick before I do it again."

He shook his head, answered the call, and put it on speaker, shooting me a pleading look. "Hey, Lukas. How can I help you?"

"I'm going to need you to meet up with the cleanup crew and follow them to the house."

Phil's eyebrow arched as he shifted into 'word mode'.. "Okay. Is there an ETA for that?"

"Lukas Reginald, tell me you are *not* on the phone with Phil right now."

The angry tone of Quinn's voice in the background had me reaching over and pulling a pillow to my face to muffle my laughter.

"Not that that's any of your concern, but I am." Lukas's voice was a bit quieter, as if he'd covered the microphone slightly.

Quinn is going to make him pay for that.

She continued, "You know where he is and who he's with. I told you that fifteen minutes ago. Is it really that much of an emergency that you couldn't wait until they come up here to eat dinner?"

The pillow did nothing to muffle my cackling.

"Is that Chelsea?"

I bit my lip and glanced up to see Phil doing the same. "It is. She's right next to me."

"I see."

Silence.

I tightened my core around him again, and Phil bit his lip as his eyes went wide and tried so very hard to keep the groan at bay. Smirking, I rocked my hips, and he took a deep breath, shooting an apologetic look my way. "So, the ETA on me heading out?" He was trying so hard to wrap up the phone conversation.

Someone cleared their throat in the background. There was a muffled scrape, what sounded like a phone being rubbed against fabric, and some muffled voices before Lukas spoke again. "Apparently we can discuss that when you come up here. Quinn says dinner will be ready in a half hour." The call abruptly ended.

I exploded in a fit of laughter. "Oh, man. Quinn is going to kill that man." When I was able to breathe normally again, I leaned down to kiss him. "Do you want to give this another go, or did that call kill the mood too much?"

He pulled my face toward his, kissed me until I leaned back to breathe, and thrusted his hips up in answer. "Nothing could make me *not* want to be inside of you."

"Good answer."

He had to work a little harder to make it happen in the short-ened timeline, but Phil had me calling out his name twice in ecstasy before finding his release. After catching our breaths, we made ourselves presentable and were upstairs with one minute to spare.

Quinn winked at me when I walked into the main area upstairs. "I'm sorry, and you're welcome."

Chapter Eighteen

Phil

Much to my surprise, Lukas didn't join us for dinner.

Quinn caught me glancing down the hallway to where I knew where his office was and rolled her eyes. "He's staying in there for now."

The tone of her voice had none of its usual cheerfulness.

"By his choice or yours?"

Quinn snickered at Chelsea's candid response. "A little bit of both. Every once in a while I need to remind him I'm not one of his little soldiers." She glanced at me. "No offense, Phil."

I chuckled. "None taken. If it wasn't you holding him accountable, it would be his sister."

A smile tugged at the corner of her mouth. "True."

My phone buzzed.

Lukas: < We need to finalize cleanup plans. ETA? >

"Everything okay?"

I glanced up to see both Chelsea and Quinn watching me, one woman looked concerned, and the other looked ready for a fight.

"Oh yeah. I'm... Quinn, I'm just going to say I'm in awe of you, and more than a little afraid of the power you wield."

She let out a deep chuckle. "Glad to see you have a functioning brain to go with those good looks."

There's a loaded sentence. "I try my best. But God help the people who ever try to rise up against this family. It's not going to be the men they have to worry about."

Chelsea raised her glass and smirked at me. "Hear, hear!"

I quickly finished dinner and headed off to Lukas's office. Quinn might have immunity from him, but I didn't. After knocking twice, I walked in. "Hey."

Lukas glanced up and nodded. "I know this isn't typical, but I really need you to meet the cleanup team. I want coverage on them, and Peter and Ryan are already busy at the lodge."

Right to business, then. I nodded. "I can do that. When should I head out?"

"Fifteen minutes enough time to prep? Ryan will be sending the details about the crew shortly."

"That'll work. I'll ask Chelsea if there's anything else I need to grab while I'm there." I turned to leave the office.

"Phil?"

I stopped and turned around. "Yeah?"

Lukas glanced past me at the door, staring at it for a moment before looking at me again. "I... apologize for interrupting earlier."

It took a lot of willpower not to show my stunned and then amused reaction to the apology. "No harm done."

My boss and friend grumbled something under his breath, but I knew better than to ask for clarification. I had a sneaky suspicion this apology was Quinn driven.

After taking a deep breath, I let it out slowly. "I'll keep you updated on the cleanup." And without waiting for a response, I headed out of his office.

Quinn and Chelsea were in the living room, sitting on the

couch and chatting, but both of their heads popped up and looked my way as soon as I walked in.

Chelsea stood up and walked over to me. "Everything okay?"

I nodded. "Yep. I need to head out in a few to do something for him, and then I'll be back."

Quinn narrowed her eyes at me. "Was he *polite*?"

A smirk tugged at my lips. "Yes he was. He even apologized, if that's what you'd like to know."

A pleased expression filled her face as she relaxed into the couch again. "It is. Thank you."

I nodded. "Glad to help. Well, don't let me interrupt girl time. I'm going to head down to get ready." I was barely half-way down the stairs when I heard someone behind me. When I got to the bottom stop, I turned around and smiled when I saw Chelsea making her way down the steps.

She stopped two from the bottom, making us eye to eye in height, and draped her arms around my shoulders. "Where are you going?"

"Your place."

"Why?" There was no missing the sudden flash of fear in her eyes.

I slid my hands around her waist, loving that she followed me downstairs. "Lukas wants me to cover the team he has coming in to clean up the townhouse. Speaking of. Can you check the suitcase I packed for you to see if there's anything else you need? I did my best to grab all the essentials, but I'm sure there's something I missed. Everything will be closed by the time I'm out of there, but I can take you to the store tomorrow if you need anything or I—"

Chelsea leaned forward and kissed me gently. "You're adorable when you ramble. I know I can get stuff from the store tomorrow. I can also order things from this wonderful invention called the Internet that I can use to place orders with other stores."

She patted my cheek. "You let me worry about my stuff so you can get ready to do your protection thing. Okay?"

I knew she was being a bit patronizing, but I'd earned that fair and square. "Okay. And I'm sorry."

A smug grin appeared on her face. "As long as you come back in one piece, all is forgiven."

It was distracting as hell to see Chelsea put her suitcase on my bed and pull things out of it. As I pulled out a clean pair of dark jeans and dark gray Henley, my attention kept going back to her, especially when she made a surprised squeak.

"Phil!"

The deep red on her face had me assuming she found one of the personal toys I'd packed. "Yes?"

"I... I'm a little surprised you packed this."

I turned toward her and pulled my shirt off. "What did I pack?"

She was adorable standing there, clearly torn between being upset, embarrassed, and amused as hell. "You know what you packed, mister. I'm not mad about it... I... I just... Why were you in *that* drawer of all places?"

I pulled the clean shirt on. "Honestly? I was looking through drawers to make sure I had all the basics covered. Socks, underwear, deodorant, that kind of thing. When I stumbled upon your *little toy*, I figured it wouldn't hurt anything to include it. I know how expensive they can get."

Chelsea's mouth dropped open, and then a sly grin replaced it as I changed into jeans. "I'm both surprised and impressed you know that." She let out a slow breath and went back to sorting through her things.

"I'm going to load up. Should I kiss you now, or do it when I'm about to head out?"

She gave me a curious look. "Why the options?"

I shrugged. "I didn't know how comfortable you would be kissing me after I'm all locked and loaded."

Chelsea rounded the end of the bed and wrapped her arms around my wait. "Sweetie, you're *always* locked and loaded." She leaned back and grabbed a bicep in each hand. "I mean, check out these guns."

Unable and not wanting to stop myself, I pulled her tight to my chest and kissed her until she let out a quiet moan. "I'll say see you later, now." I kissed her again. "Try not to worry, and don't feel like you have to wait up for me. I have no idea how long this is going to take."

I saw the tension rise in her eyes almost as much as I felt it in her muscles.

She laid her head on my chest and let out a strained sigh. "I'll do my best. There's a strong possibility I might be partaking in some alcohol tonight."

"There's wine and beer in the fridge and liquor in the cabinet next to it. Feel free to have whatever you want. Invite Quinn down, too, if you want. She could be a good distraction."

"Okay." Chelsea tipped her head up again and slid her arms around my neck to pull me down for a kiss. "You be careful, or I'll kick your ass."

I grinned at the gorgeous spitfire of a woman in my arms. "Yes, ma'am."

Relief washed over me twenty minutes later when I confirmed the license plate on the truck in front of me matched the number Ryan gave me. *One less problem.* The two people who hopped out of the cab were exactly who he said they would be, too, and I felt slightly less on edge about the evening.

. . .

Phil: < Made it to Chelsea's - cleanup team is here - all good so far. >
   Lukas: < Excellent. >
   Phil: < Heading in. >

The man stepped forward first and held his hand out for me to shake. "I'm Guy, and this is Annie."

I shook both their hands. "Phil. You two have done this before?"

Annie nodded and patted her thigh, where I noticed a small gun holstered. "Yep. You aren't the first of our clients to request this type of cleanup, and this isn't the first time your boss has hired us. Shall we get started?"

After confirming the truck was, in fact, empty, I made a lap around the building and was pleased to see nothing of concern. *Now for the mess.* I gestured for the duo to follow me toward the front door. I unlocked it, pushed it open, and immediately held my arm out.

"What's up?"

I shook my head and pulled out my phone. "This isn't how I left the entry a few hours ago." After taking a few photos and sending them to the guys, I walked in, careful not to step on the two sets of bloody boot prints on the light gray tiles.

Phil: < These weren't here earlier. >

"If the footprints here are new, what's the status of the blood on the stairs?" Guy's deep voice pulled my attention from my phone.

I glanced up and noticed a distinct trail of crimson. *Shit.* "Nope. That's new, too." Immediately pulling out my gun, I made my way to the stairs and flipped on the light. Nothing. Not that I'd been expecting much.

"The kitchen's clear."

I nodded at Annie's words. "Thanks."

Guy appeared in my peripheral. "I'll be behind you."

Once again careful to avoid stepping on the blood, I crept up the stairs, never taking my eyes off the bathroom and bedroom doors.

I cleared the bathroom while Guy checked the closet. When I turned on the light in Chelsea's room, I froze. "Fuck."

"Trouble?"

"Missing cargo." I eased into the room, looking for anything else missing or out of place. The floor wasn't the only thing missing evidence. The duct tape and syringe that had been on top of the dresser were gone, too.

I pulled out my phone, disregarded the texts, and called Lukas. "We have a problem. Sylas is gone."

There was a moment of silence. "I'm sorry, *what*?"

"He's not here."

"I thought you took care of that problem. You said he was as good as dead."

Shaking my head, I let out a frustrated breath. "I thought he was. There was barely a pulse when you told me to clear out earlier. I can't prove he left alive, but he most certainly isn't here. The syringe isn't here, either."

"You cleared the rest of the place?"

"Yeah. Guy and Annie helped me."

Lukas sighed. "Be as quick as you can. One of us will drive over and watch the outside until all of you are done."

"Will do." I ended the call and slid the phone back in my pocket.

"One less thing to dispose of?"

I smirked at Guy. "Yep. Looks like it."

He nodded. "Well, we'll get to it, then."

With that, he left and headed back downstairs.

Wait. There were text messages.

I pulled my phone back out.

Chelsea: < Well, since you're not afraid of what you found earlier, could you grab the rest of my stash? >

Chelsea: < Also, I'd love to have the entire contents of my bathroom vanity. If you can. >

Chelsea: < I have another suitcase in the back of the hall closet. >

Chelsea: < you'd better still be careful. <3 >

The little heart emoji on the end put the biggest grin on my face, until I reread the first message and realized what she wanted me to bring.

I glanced over at the drawer in question. *What else is buried in there?*

Once I'd happily finished packing the things Chelsea had requested, I headed downstairs with the suitcase in hand.

Annie raised an eyebrow and smirked, bucket and cleaning supplies in hand. "Taking a trip?"

I shook my head, amused. "No. The owner politely requested for me to grab a few things while I was here."

"That's kind of you. Speaking of packing, you might want to take a look at what's under bucket number one. We found it after picking up the couch, and no, neither of us touched it."

My attention went to the upside down bucket on the floor. "You shouldn't have. I didn't get you anything."

She snickered and headed upstairs. Guy was just walking back in from taking something out to the truck. "Annie tell you about the bucket?"

"She did." I walked over and picked it up. "Oh. That's *not* what I was expecting." Crouching down, I once again took my phone out and took a few pictures.

Phil: < Quick question. Do you own a gun? >
Chelsea: < What? No. Why? >
Phil: < We found one. I'm going to call Ryan. >
Phil: < and I am being careful. >

I sent Ryan and Lukas the photos before immediately calling Ryan.

"I'm assuming this call has something to do with the photos that just popped on my phone?"

I chuckled. "Yep. Chelsea said she didn't own a gun when I asked her. I also don't think she would have left it under the couch."

"What?" The verbal explosion from him didn't surprise me.

"Yep. Annie and Guy found it when they moved the couch out."

"What the…" Ryan let out a deep sigh. "Do you have gloves and a plastic bag with you?"

"Of course. I'm assuming you'd like me to bag it up for you. Where am I dropping it off?"

There was a chuckle. "I'll pick it up."

I glanced toward the front door. "Are you my second shadow?"

"Yep. How's it going there?"

Standing up, I pulled latex gloves out of one of my pockets. "The destroyed things are out of the house, and Annie and Guy are upstairs working on the stains in the carpet."

"I'll be there shortly. Once you can hand it over, I can get started on figuring out who our unlucky owner is."

An hour later I was locking up Chelsea's townhouse and following the truck to a warehouse Lukas gave us the address to. There were several storage units, and once I helped offload the items, I was on my way back to the house.

My phone had buzzed a few times, and most of them had been Chelsea filling me in on her night and the fun she was having with Quinn.

The most recent one was from Lukas.

Lukas: < Come straight to my office when you get back. >

Great.

I wasn't surprised when Ryan's car was already in the driveway. Making sure I was quiet when I walked in, I literally tiptoed into Lukas's office.

Ryan glanced up from his laptop. "Are you hunting rabbits, or something?"

"I didn't know where the ladies were and didn't want to alert them that I was home. Chelsea was really worried when I headed out earlier. Speaking of, any leads about who owns the gun?"

Lukas snickered. "Actually, we know *exactly* who it belongs to, but wanted you here before we called her up."

I tipped my head to the side. "Why?"

"One, I'm pretty sure she will feel better knowing you're okay. Two, and this is probably the more significant reason, I'm not sure how she's going to react to the name."

Interesting. "Do you want me to get her?"

Lukas set down his phone. "I just asked Quinn to send her in."

Moments later, there was a soft knock on the door, followed by it opening and Chelsea poking her head in. "Quinn said you wan— Phil!" She burst into the room, ran at me, and wrapped her arms around my waist. "I thought something happened to you and that's why they called me up here." Chelsea turned toward Lukas and pointed at him. "Don't scare me like that! Just because I know who you are doesn't mean I won't lay into you like I did your dumbass brother."

"I'm sorry, Chelsea. Phil literally just walked in when I texted you."

She glared at him and then let out a deep sigh. "It's a good thing I like your girlfriend."

Ryan tried to cough over his snicker. None of us bought it.

I sat down in one of the leather chairs, and Chelsea immediately sat in my lap. "Comfy?"

She nodded. "Very much so."

Ryan cleared his throat. "Chelsea, do you know someone named Reid Garrison White?"

Every muscle in her back went rigid. "I know a guy named Garrison. Why? How do *you* know that name? Wait. Phil asked me about a gun. Are they related? What's going on?"

I rubbed her back in hope it would help relax her. "I found an abandoned gun at your place while it was being cleaned."

"What? Why was his gun there? Was he in my house? How did he even get in there?" Chelsea looked at me. "The only gun that's even been in my house, well, that I've known about, is whatever Phil's walked in with."

I was still pissed about someone getting back in the house. "I locked that door behind me. I double checked it before leaving."

Lukas nodded. "Good to know. But back to this Reid guy. How do you know him?"

Chelsea took a deep breath and let it out slowly. "Well, if it's the same guy, and I have a feeling it is, I was introduced to him as Garrison, not Reid. He was with Sylas the first night he threatened me. Garrison was *all* about June that night." She shifted to look at me. "Garrison wasn't as pushy as Sylas, and didn't run his mouth, but I still got some weird vibes from him. He was nice enough to her, but she can do so much better."

Lukas nodded again. "And how are they connected?"

"They are allegedly best friends. June and I were told

Garrison was visiting from out of town and that it had been years since they'd gotten together."

Ryan was already furiously typing away on his computer.

"Anything else?" I didn't like how worked up and tense Chelsea still was, and wanted to get her out of here and make her feel better.

Chelsea

Lukas had barely dismissed us when Phil had me out of the office and back in his room. I had no complaints about it. There was more going on than the guys talked about while I was in there, but at this point I didn't care. All I cared about was holding onto Phil. Today had been a lot, and I wanted and needed the reassurance that he was okay and I was safe.

"Chels, what do you need? You've been wound up since they dropped his name."

I let out a deep sigh and leaned against him. "I just need you."

He kissed the top of my head. "I'm right here, sweetheart. I'm not letting you go unless you want me to, and I might not do it even then."

"Can we at least get in bed? I'm not sure if I can sleep just yet, but the cuddles would be appreciated."

"We can do anything you want. I'm going to shower, change real fast, and be right back, okay?" He stared into my eyes with those intense and beautiful brown eyes, leaving me nearly breathless. "Are you going to be okay?"

I nodded. He closed the door behind him after walking out, and it took me a second before I could move. *Pajamas. Right.*

By the time he was back, I was dressed in boy-shorts and one of his t-shirts, and was snuggled into his bed. I wanted to be surrounded by everything that smelled like him.

A pleased and proud expression spread across his face as he walked into the room and looked me over.

"What?" I glanced around, feeling immediately self-conscious.

Phil sat down on the bed. "It caught me off guard how much I liked seeing you in my bed when I walked in. I'd happily get used to it."

"Sounds like you get to enjoy the view for at least another night or two since my place got trashed."

His smile waned for a moment before crawling under the blankets and snuggling up next to me. "You can stay here as long as you want."

My heart skipped a beat at the thought. "What about Peter... and Lukas and Quinn?"

He sighed. "You need somewhere to stay until we've tracked down Garrison and made sure your place is safe and able to be lived in again. Also, no one is going to kick you out of my room."

"If you say so."

Phil laid on his back and I draped myself over him. He ran his hand up and down my back for what felt like hours before I even started to feel tired. Neither one of us said a word, and eventually sleep claimed me.

The next morning I found myself in an empty bed. Trying to shove down my disappointment, I reached for my phone and felt better seeing text messages waiting for me.

Phil: < Good morning. I kissed you before I left, but you didn't budge. I hope you slept well. >

Frank: < Lukas and Phil filled me in. You're off today. >

I just about threw the phone across the room. *Quinn was only forced to take days off when something actually happened to her.* With a huff, I flipped the blanket off me and got out of bed, grabbing one of Phil's hoodies on the way out.

"Good morning, sunshine."

I froze in place. "What are you doing down here?"

Quinn smirked as she took a sip of whatever was in her mug. "Other than the fact I live here? I apparently have the day off with you." She slid a mug over as I sat next to her. "Here."

"What's this?"

"My take on Edith's hot chocolate, but in coffee form."

After taking a sip, my eyebrows shot up. "Is there even coffee in this?"

"There was when I started." The irritated expression on my friend's face darkened. "It was a long night."

Cautiously, I took another sip. "Do I want to know?"

Quinn let out a deep sigh and stared at me. The intensity of her stare froze me in place. "You know? Yeah. Fuck it. I'm going to explode if I don't tell someone."

She never drops the F bomb. "Oh?"

After another long drink of her doctored-up coffee, Quinn set down her mug. "I overheard more of a conversation than Lukas thought I did, and..." She let out another sigh. "Apparently the danger hasn't passed yet. And not only that, but some of it appears to be making its way to Chicago."

"So what does that mean for us?"

"We're housemates for the foreseeable future."

I stared off in front of me, trying to process. "This is so much bigger than some idiot showing up at my house with the intent to knock me out and abduct me, isn't it?"

Quinn nodded. "Yep."

"Lukas and his guys are going to be able to keep everyone safe, right?"

"That's the plan they're working on now."

I bit my lip as worry crept in. "This isn't going to be a quick thing, is it?"

She shook her head. "I have a feeling things are going to get a lot crazier before they finally settle down."

Oh boy.

Find out what happens next in *Pretty Much Screwed*

Pretty Much Screwed (Book #3)

Jess and Connor's story.

The last thing Jessica Barlowe wants is a professional babysitter. What does she end up with? An entire security detail. It isn't the first time her life has been in some kind of danger, but when your best friend practically begs you to humor her, what's a girl to do? How bad could it be?

When Connor Valesteri is told he is going to be heading the security detail for his boss's sister's best friend, he takes it as the ultimate compliment, until he meets her. Jess challenges him like no one else and pushes back on the restrictions placed on her.

As Connor starts to see through Jess's tough exterior, her dangerous combination of brains and beauty might be too much to resist. For Jess, having a gorgeous, respectful second shadow might not be so bad. A man that actually *sees* her, and leaves her feeling defenseless and empowered at the same time.

When threats and attacks come from every direction, tension runs high. Jess and Connor must figure out how to navigate attempts on their lives, betrayals, and each other before they reach a breaking point that forces tough decisions to be made before moving forward.

Damaging information surfaces from an unlikely source, causing her entire world to crumble around her, will the truth surface in time? Can he save her, or will the haunting memories of her past come to life and cost her everything?

Locked and Loaded (Book #4)
Ryan and Ellen's story.

After an epic betrayal that shakes up the Agostis, Ryan is scrambling to help keep things together. He has to be on top of it, or the people he loves will get hurt.

Ellen is also struggling with parental pressure to find a "suitable man", but her eyes are firmly set on someone who is everything she's ever wanted.

Danger brought them together, chemistry kept them together, but will life tear them apart?

About the Author

Hey everyone and welcome to my little corner of the world. I'm glad you're here! I'm just a quirky, nerdy lady writing stories that are begging to be put on paper. I live in an adorable, little town in Indiana with my amazing husband, our adorable daughter, and our two cats. When I'm not holed up in my office, you can find me reading, drinking coffee and tea, hanging out with my family and friends, baking, working on DIY projects around the house, and playing D&D.

I have been obsessed with reading and writing from a very young age. Growing up, it was all about The Baby Sitter Club and then Harry Potter and then The Arrows of the Queen. I started writing my first novel in high school, my second novel in college, and after teaching for a while and starting a family, I decided to tackle the dream of becoming an author. The rest is history.

You'll find my bookshelves filled with everything from YA to historical fiction to romance to classics to sci-fi and fantasy to mental health. It's a mixed bag and I wouldn't have it any other way.

I hope to see you around!

You can find out more about me and my work at: www.emgarner.net

www.ingramcontent.com/pod-product-compliance
Lightning Source LLC
Chambersburg PA
CBHW060642260626
47161CB00008B/2962